The Scattergun Men

The Scattergun Men

LAURAN PAINE

Sagebrush

Large Print Westerns

Library of Congress Cataloging-in-Publication Data

Paine, Lauran.
   The scattergun men / Lauran Paine.
      p.   cm.
   ISBN 1-57490-382-9 (lg. print : hardcover)
   1. Large type books. I. Title

Due to recent problems with the mail, complete Library of
Congress Cataloging-in-Publication Data was not available at
the time of publication.

Libraries should call (800) 818-7574 and we will fax or mail
the CIP Data upon request.

Cataloging in Publication Data is available from
the British Library and the National Library of Australia.

Sagebrush Large Print Westerns are published in the United
States and Canada by Thomas T. Beeler, Publisher, PO Box 659,
Hampton Falls, New Hampshire 03844-0659. ISBN 1-57490-382-9

Published in the United Kingdom, Eire, and the Republic of
South Africa by Isis Publishing Ltd, 7 Centremead, Osney
Mead, Oxford OX2 0ES England. ISBN 0-7531-6632-1

Published in Australia and New Zealand by Bolinda Publishing
Pty Ltd, 17 Mohr Street, Tullamarine, Victoria, Australia, 3043
ISBN 1-74030-649-X

Manufactured by Sheridan Books in Chelsea, Michigan.

The Scattergun Men

CHAPTER ONE

THE BOAT CAPTAIN SAID, "I DON'T WANT NO SICKNESS on the craft. If the boy's ailing I'll put the lot of you ashore at the next landing."

Reuben, the big oaken one, full of anguish now and troubled, scarcely even heard the captain. It was his boy, Jonas, who was sweaty and queasy. Reuben had cause to be fearful. There was cholera on the river, folks said. It carried off a whole band of Mandan redskins last fall, squaws, bucks and pups.

Reuben stood there, big fists knotted, as helpless as only a big powerful man can be in the fact of something all his power couldn't turn aside. But Bob, still seated on the tarred coil of rope, whittling on a riverbank willow twig, exactly the way he'd been three hours earlier at daybreak, said, "Cap'n; what's the next landing?"

The bull-boat skipper was a squatty, gnarled, massive man running a little to tallow about the girth, black-eyed and black-haired, and so it was rumoured, black-hearted to boot. His name was Hazen Garrity and folks called him Cap'n Haze.

"Wood landin'," he growled, resenting having to say that because wood landings only meant there was a rickety wharf and cord-wood cut and stacked to be sold to the Missouri River boatmen coming up or going down. Wood landings usually had just one person, the attendant. They were different from town landings, all the same Cap'n Haze had no intention of floating those Kentucky spindle-shanks on upriver where their feverish brat would spread his sickness, whatever it

1

was—maybe the cholera—so's folks would trace it back to his boat and maybe lynch him.

Bob said, still slowly whittling with his head down, his face hidden by the old floppy-brimmed hat, "Cap'n; where'd a sick child get care at a wood landin' ?"

" 'Tain't my concern," said Garrity. "I just got a rule—no sick uns. Male, female, old, young, broad or lean. No sick uns on my boat."

"Well now, Cap'n," said lanky young Bob, flipping the riverbank willow twig over into the sucking, chocolate river as it lapped along rearward, "a man'd hardly do that to a sick dog, let alone a human bein'— set 'em off where there wasn't anythin' but woods."

"I would," said Cap'n Haze. "And I've done it too, emigrant. I've done it more'n once."

Bob straightened up on his coil of tarred rope. He was rawboned with prominent cheekbones and eyes the color of a summertime harvest sky; pale as clear water and as flawless as glass. He didn't smile; in fact Little Bob as the folks called him, although he stood six-two in his bare feet, had forgotten how to smile. He reared up and gazed over at Cap'n Haze with that blank, totally expressionless boyish face, and didn't utter another word. Reuben didn't see that look or he'd have been warned. Reuben didn't see anything, really, but a grey-flowing continuity of days and nights on the move with his wife and son and younger brother, across land, over mountains, through towns, camping in rags along the creek bottoms, eating whatever their guns brought down, until now they were on the last leg of it. Up the Missouri to Montana. Out of the 'States into the territories. Hoping and praying it was all true what men had said back in Kentucky, that a willing man with courage could make himself free of

2

everything and everybody, up in Montana Territory.

None of it had been easy, Old Ephraim had told them, before they departed, "I'll stay back, boys, an' directly you'll be back here. When I was your age Kaintuck was wilderness too, but I've seed it change an' I expect at m'age I'd be foolish to see what's on t'other side of any more mountains. I'll hang back and see you ride back down the pike a year or two from now."

Old Ephraim hadn't been their father. Nor the uncle. Old Eph had been the sheriff who'd auctioned off their farm and livestock and utensils after their maw died to satisfy debts.

The Missouri River was an oily rope of wet steel about musket-shot across, with the smell of decay to it most fresh-water rivers had. When the wind was good Cap'n Haze's filthy old sail would fetch them along at a smart enough clip considering the craft was a bull-boat—which meant it sort of sidled back and forth because it had no keel. But when the wind failed Cap'n Haze'd put in to shore, tie up to a tree, and set out his fishy-lines until the wind returned.

It was a slow way of getting north. It was also the cheapest way to get their wagons and critters and belongings from Independence on up-country, so Reuben strained ahead in spirit, or spent his time below in the reeking little dirty cabin with Eulalia his wife, fretting over their child, or tried to urge Cap'n Haze along.

Little Bob whittled. The third day out Eulalia told Reuben his brother was going to fade away to a shadow if he didn't eat more. Little Bob told them to bring the child above decks. The air was cleaner, he said, and besides, youngsters forgot their miseries when they saw racoons along the riverbanks, or bluejays scolding in the

3

high trees, or the shapes clouds formed into as they ran forever across the curved immensity of the north-country heavens.

Eulalia brought him up. Reuben got down and for all his immense size, was gentle as making the little nest of ticking coverlets for the child to lie in. Reuben even rigged a little texas for the boy so the sun wouldn't directly hit him.

Little Bob whittled him a horse and he smiled about that. He vomited once in the morning, twice in the afternoon, and sometime in the night his heart broke under the strain of a silent convulsion. In the morning Eulalia's scream told whittling Little Bob on his coil of tarred rope what he'd known was going to happen since the day before.

Cap'n Haze put in an hour early that evening so they could take the ticking-bundle back a piece from the river and bury it in a quiet dell. When they returned late, Cap'n Haze was already asleep up for'ard, at peace finally, because he'd felt fearful right from the start when the child had turned up ill.

Reuben stayed below with Eulalia all the following day. The chores on board were tended to by Little Bob. When they put in the next night Cap'n Haze said two more days and they'd be into the Territory. He grinned at Little Bob and sucked on his pipe, yellow spittle on his chin. "You'll know it. For a hunnert miles there's nothin' but land. No mountains, no hills, no forests, just grass. A sea of grass, emigrant, as far as you can see, once you get back a piece from the river."

Little Bob whittled. First, it had been a wagon. Next it had been an arrow. Then it had been the wooden horse, and now it was a miniature shotgun with the barrels purposefully shortened.

4

"I tell you, emigrant, the urge to land has been right powerful this year. They been a-comin' like ants since early spring. An' like you folks, they been a-buryin' a few along the riverbanks, too. An' later on I expect the Sioux an' Crow and Blackfeet will take their toll; they always have. Ahhh; but emigrant, it's the Northern Cheyenne. Now there's a real fightin' redskin. You put a Northern Cheyenne an' a Sioux together with their signs right an' their weepons loaded, an' gawd-a'mercy, emigrant, there's nothin' worse, not even the cholera."

Little Bob leaned back, pushed his wicked-bladed big knife into its scabbard, sewn into the top of his right boot on the outside where it was right handy, and gazed with those very light, clear eyes of his at Hazen Garrity. Little Bob was a right quiet man, normally; had been right quiet since he'd been small and had watched them bury his paw first, then his maw, and later on, Old Ned his dog. Back home folks had said Little Bob never smiled. They said he was too sensitive for his own good. It may have been true, but when Little Bob had been seventeen—six years back—he'd done something which had shocked even the Kentuckians. He'd challenged a bullying older man to a gunfight in the center of the road of their hamlet, and had shown up lugging a double-barrel shotgun. He stood a hundred feet away and cut his adversary literally in two with both barrels; it was the goriest killing folks had ever seen.

Sensitive, maybe, they muttered, but there was a sight more to Little Bob than just being sensitive. There was something leashed up inside him that was enough to make brave men sidestep.

Reuben, folks said, was totally different. He was as strong as two men and oaken in his convictions, surely, but

5

he was a gentle, soft-spoken, tolerant man who made friends and stood staunch in his ways of what was right and wrong. Mighty Reuben was a reasoning man. He'd had his share of fights, but Reuben only battered his adversaries senseless; he didn't gouge the eyes nor stove in the ribs with his boots, nor twist arms until they snapped. Folks back in Kentucky had said Reuben would rather go reason with an enemy than fight him. Not Little Bob though. He'd listen to all a man had to say, then he'd slice through all the words to the very core of the matter, and call his enemy on that alone. He was very practical. Deacon Witherspoon back home once said Little Bob's trouble was that he didn't have a shred of illusion about anything. Not about man or the Devil, nor even about God, and that was a terrible way for a man to be, because it chained him to the earth and the earth's treacherous creatures alone, for if a man couldn't find some good in everything, he was doomed to walk forever the paths of violence and harshness.

Possibly the Deacon had been right. At least Little Bob sat there on his coiled rope gazing at Cap'n Haze as though his glass-clear eyes saw right through to the core of the man. As though he had laid bare the greed, the slothfulness, the sly watchfulness, and the delight Haze Garrity took in bedevilling folks whom he considered less respectable than himself.

And perhaps Little Bob did see Garrity as he really was, for he turned, finally, to gaze along the riverbank, shutting out the bull-boat skipper from his mind as cleanly as though he'd used that razor-sharp big knife to make the incision.

But Cap'n Haze wasn't finished yet. He saw from the side of his eye that he had made no impression at all upon the lanky, grave Kentuckian. That rankled. Haze

6

Garrity was one of those men who could stand anything except being ignored. He liked his emigrants to writhe a little, to turn pale and fearful at the grisly tales he told of Montana Territory.

"If the redskins don't make a run on you," he went on, "the cowmen will. If there's anythin' cowmen despise an' loathe, it's emigrants come out here to build their shacks and sew their bean patches on good grazin' land. They sometimes shoot folks for that. An' burn 'em out or tie 'em to trees and whip 'em to ribbons. I'm tellin' you, emigrant, so's you'll know. So's the lady down below'll understand that if she figures her tears'll be done with when she gets over losin' the sick kid, she's dead wrong."

Little Bob leaned with his back to the superstructure, still impassively watching the riverbank go past. The only time he moved was when a cloud-shadow passed along, briefly shading his section of the big sky, and mottling the river below. It was a limitless land, this northern country, with fewer and fewer trees and more and more rolling miles of waving grass. Those cloud-shadows, he'd soon learn, were part of every day, sometimes large, sometimes small, but always moving over the immense emptiness which was Montana Territory. He could appreciate, just by watching the land form up and take on its distinctiveness, that only mounted men survived up here. A man on foot was dwarfed down to ant-size. He had eleven hundred dollars in little gold coins next to his belly in a money-belt; somewhere up here he'd find just the horse a man'd need to hunt and travel across this empty world of hush and loneliness.

Something deep down stirred in Little Bob; something free and softly exulting. There was nothing

7

here; a man made his own environment, his own life, and that was how it should be. If there was a God, this is where He'd meet Bob Tollman, where the world was new, the sky clean, the forests rolled back so a man could see Him face to face, standing on his own two feet.

He arose and walked away from Cap'n Haze; went for'ard to gaze at his big new world.

CHAPTER TWO

IT REQUIRED A HALF DAY FOR THEM TO OFF-LOAD, AND Cap'n Haze didn't lift a hand, not even when grey and dull-eyed Eulalia struggled down the plank to the willow-bank shore with their ticking-quilts. The horses were gaunt but glad to be on solid land once again. The old wagon was ready, too, for they'd taken turns dragging the wheels alongside in the water so the wood would swell tight to the tyres.

Reuben went down to the bank when all was ready to have his reckoning with Cap'n Haze while Little Bob finished the hitching.

"Thirty-five," said big Reuben in his soft-booming voice, counting out the silver dollars into Cap'n Haze's callused palm.

"That was before I had to make extra stops, like buryin' the kid," said the bull-boat skipper. "I'll have to have another ten for all that, emigrant."

Reuben stood gazing at the coins in his hand for a moment, then brought up his dark blue eyes. "We didn't hold you up any," he said gravely. "Captain; you stopped when an' where you liked; sometimes you stopped to fish when there was yet a couple of hours o' daylight."

8

Cap'n Haze bared his teeth. "All a riverboat man's got to sell is his time, emigrant, an' he's damned well entitled to his wages. I say you owe me . . ." Haze turned. Little Bob had silently walked down there. He was standing ten feet behind and to one side, his prominent cheekbones making his clear, smoldering stare very noticeable. There wasn't a particle of warmth in those eyes right now. Not a particle. Bob had a double-barrel shotgun with sawed-off barrels drooping from one arm. Cap'n Haze said, "You're robbin' me, the both of you, but all right, keep the ten dollars." He leered and turned to go back up his plank. "When the redskins and cowmen get through, you're goin' to wish a hunnert times you'd give me that ten—and thirty more as well—to take you back out of this Montana country."

They left the river, travelling slowly because the horses weren't strong. But the land favored them. It was level to rolling. Now and then they'd spy a tree, usually in a little gully or upon some greeny sidehill where shallow sub-surface moisture allowed it to flourish, but mostly all they saw was stirrup-high rolling grass, sometimes cornhusk yellow, sometimes buckskin-tan, depending upon which way the breeze bent its tops.

Because they were rural people their thoughts ran to the perils of a land like this, foremost of which, in their minds, was the danger of fire. If this endless prairie caught fire and wind came, no horse on earth could outrun death. The first night they quietly discussed this. It was Reuben who had the solution.

"If a man plow a wide row and left it lie fallow, then plowed it again each spring just when the growth was comin' on, directly he'd have himself a firebreak."

The second day they saw a dustcloud moving parallel to them but miles southward. Little Bob took the saddle

9

critter and rode down for a cautious look, his scattergun lightly balancing across his lap.

It was a migrating tribe of Indians. The bucks rode slightly apart with their lances and shields and bedaubed ponies. Behind them came the squaws and children and endlessly fighting dogs. The noise back there was fierce as old grandmothers lashed left and right at both dogs and black-eyed, moon-faced children. In the rear of the straggling mob were the young boys, well mounted, bringing along the horse herd.

Kentucky had redmen too, but not like these. In Kentucky the redmen went to school right along with the whites; they wore britches and shirts and hats. They went to church and read books. These were different; the bucks had no seats in their leggings, their bodies were bare from the waist up, and they were armed to the gills. When he wearied of watching, Little Bob returned. After that either he or Reuben kept watch at night around their camp, and by day scouted on ahead. But they encountered no more redskins.

On the seventh day with their misery along the Missouri nearly buried under layers of fresh new things they'd encountered, they spied a little band of horsemen atop a low, straw-colored knoll, watching them.

"Emigrants like us, more'n likely," suggested Reuben. Eulalia said nothing, but she never took her eyes off those men on their little knoll, sitting up there as still and silent as Indians. Little Bob kept his own counsel. Emigrants or something altogether different, he had the shotgun across the saddle with him.

"They're comin' down," he called back, and reined his saddle animal around so that he'd intercept the strangers before they reached the wagon.

There were six of them, heavily armed, bearded and

shaggy. One was a huge man, nearly as broad and massive as Reuben. This one held up his hand. He was wearing gauntlets of the whitest buckskin Little Bob had ever seen, with intricate beadwork on the upper part. His rifle was sheathed in a fancy buckskin case also, but with fringes. This one was smiling but the other five were silently impassive as they halted looking beyond Little Bob to the wagon and its occupants.

The big one dropped his arm and said, "Howdy, stranger," to Little Bob, who nodded back without speaking. "Emigrants, eh? Well; keep headin' in the direction you're goin' an' you'll come to Indian Springs Valley. Best land in Montana Territory." The man broadly smiled, turned and loped eastward in the direction of the river without casting another glance towards the wagon.

Little Bob watched as the others swung away behind their spokesman, then he turned and nodded to Reuben, the wagon lurched, squealed for want of axle grease, and went bumping along again. Little Bob didn't ride on down, but kept out a short ways riding parallel. He thought those six men were camp-robbers. Up and down the Missouri folks talked of camp-robbers; bands of gun-handy guerillas who'd appear as though out of thin air to rob folks, kill them too, if they resisted. But a blind camp-robber could see there was nothing in that wagon; even the canvas top was patched, the wagon itself was loose at every joint, and the horses were wolf-bait critters.

At their camp that night Eulalia said, sounding faintly hopeful, "Indian Springs Valley. It has a musical sound to it. Indian—Springs—Valley."

Reuben put goosegrease on a collar sore and worried over the worn-out shoes the horses wore, but he didn't fret aloud. He never fretted aloud. Bob had said once that Reuben'd be a sight better off if he balled up his fists now and then, reared back his head, and roared defiance at the Universe; that a man who always kept things bottled up inside him was likely to smother on his own blood someday.

On the tenth day they saw Indian Springs Valley. It struck them all the same way: Bigger than life. So vast were the surrounding distances that the valley itself seemed as large as all Kentucky to them.

There was a settlement down along a cottonwood creek; the first they'd seen in weeks. "Home," said Reuben. "Just a little longer an' he'd have seen it with us."

They drove down to a dusty set of ruts, dropped into them and after that Reuben didn't have to touch the lines until they were within rifle-shot of the town. Little Bob loped ahead; evening was coming on, they'd need a place to camp. He found it, quite a little ways below the town along the creek, went back and guided Reuben on in. It got dark early in early summer in Indian Springs Valley, but after all the silent, depthlessly lonely nights which had gone before, this one seemed to belong to another world; someone up there in the town had a piano. The music was poorly, the piano badly out of tune, but the three of them sat around their cooking-fire listening all the same. There'd been no music for them in a very long time, not even bad music.

It was a pleasant night with the overhead stars as large as rocks, as bright as diamonds, and as coldly impersonal as stars sometimes seem, depending upon how a person looks at them.

Eulalia walked out where Little Bob was caring for the horses after supper, hands folded loosely as she slow-paced the velvet night. For a while she watched the sureness of his hands, of his movements, then she gazed out and all around breathing deeply of the balmy air, and she said, "Bob; is this it?" He straightened up, turned and gazed at her. "Is this really it? It seems that we've been on the move so long, I'm uneasy about stopping." She dropped her head to meet his eyes. Eulalia was only a year older than Little Bob. She was a handsome woman; once, she'd been pretty, but hardship, suffering, grief, had brought her to maturity. Now, the round girlishness was gone; she was a handsome, tall woman, full-bodied, taffy-haired, with violet eyes the color of corn flowers, and in the silvery light of night she seemed as flawless as a carved cameo.

"It's so—different, Bob. So huge and quiet and—unknown. There are no forests, either. Is this really it? It's so different from home."

"Well," he said quietly, thoughtfully, "it's where we start looking, Eulalia. If this isn't it, we'll go on. But we start thinking about stopping now, and that's the first step."

"You're glad, Bob?"

He kept gazing at her, his pale, piercing eyes cloudy with a strange gentleness, making him look almost like his older brother, this once. "I'm glad to be here, yes. I've been a long time looking for this land." He pointed at the ground. "It's never had a plow plunged into it, Eulalia." He pointed out yonder in the western night. "No fences, no near neighbors. It's a fresh new world. A man can stand up in this place and see his life all around him, waiting to be formed into whatever he wants to make it. Back home . . ."

"Yes; back home, Bob . . . ?"

His arm fell back to his side. He looked straight at her

from beneath the brim of his old hat. "Back home—too many people. Too many rules. Too many books, too much talk."

She understood his meaning, and yet she sighed a little, for Eulalia Tollman was a woman, with all a woman's deep-down desire for security and safety and conformity. She stood a moment in silence, then she raised her violet gaze to his face and said, "Bob; would it help if we knew what the future held?"

"No; it'd hinder. This is promise and opportunity, Eulalia. It's challenge and reward."

"And Indians, Bob, and camp-robbers—and those angry cattlemen Captain Garrity talked of. Oh; I heard. I heard all he told you, back there on the river. Bob; Reuben is tired. He's older than you are. He seeks peace and quiet. We're not like you are; we're worn out from the struggling."

"Then you'll never make it here," he told her with a solid ring of conviction in his voice. "Look at it, Eulalia; open land as far as you can see. Clear air, clean scents, a brand spankin' new world waiting to be molded by men's hands. Work ahead as far as a man can figure; sweaty toil from sunup to sundown for years on end." He paused, looked at his cracked old boots, looked up at her again, and said, "What's life for, Eulalia? Since when have folks any right to expect it different? In Kaintuck or Montana Territory—folks got to labor on the land. Reuben's not worn-out; neither are you. What's ailin' the pair of you is this everlasting driving into the sunset. After awhile it becomes habit; you get up in the morning, hitch up and drive all day, un-hitch and bed down again at night. You lose sight of something; what a man's duty is on earth—to work for his old age, to make the ground yield to his hands and

14

his back. Here; we'll prosper. Here, if a man fails, he's got to look just one person in the face—himself. You understand how I feel, Eulalia? A new world without tracks or boundaries or restrictions; a place where you'n Reuben and I can put down our roots and see what kind of folks we really are. A new life for all of us."

"If Jonas had just been able to—"

"Jonas is gone, Eulalia. That's a plain fact o' life, and life is for the living. We'll always remember, but it's not a healthy thing to keep draggin' the dead out all the time. Leave Jonas in his grave."

She considered the great vault of heaven, her face tilted to the starshine, her large, soft mouth lightly closed. He watched a moment, then turned back to caring for the horses. She said, without looking at him, "Granny Hickson told me right after Reuben and I were married, that if a person lives long enough everything they've seen will come around again. We'll have no more children, Bob. The loss takes a part of you away leaving an emptiness."

He went right on working with the horses. It was almost as though she wasn't standing there. Piano music came softly and the scent of woodsmoke farther up the creek at some other camp made the night seem friendly.

"You'll have more," he said, almost off-handedly. "If you don't what's the sense of all this? A man doesn't work just for himself; he can't. I don't reckon a woman can either. You'll have more."

"And you?" she asked, dropping her eyes to his lean, bronzed face, which was handsome in its bony, high-cheekboned way; strong and honest and steady.

He paused at his work, looked across an animal's swayed back at her, and shrugged, lifting wide shoulders and dropping them. He didn't move, but

15

neither did he answer, which is the way he was about things he had no way of influencing.

"She'll come one of these days," Eulalia told him. "You'll see," then she turned and went slow-pacing back to their wagon where the coals were dying and where Reuben was asleep in their bedding inside.

The piano music stopped, eventually; the wood-smoke died away. There was a hush so deep a man could listen to the steady strong beat of his own heart. Little Bob went back to his blankets beneath the wagon and lay back taking the pulse of the night. In the heart of all this strangeness, he felt oddly at home and perfectly at peace. He closed his eyes and slept.

CHAPTER THREE

THE SETTLEMENT HAD BEEN ESTABLISHED THREE YEARS earlier as New Town, Montana Territory, but now it was known as just plain Newton.

It had tent-top stores and green-wood saloons where the sap still came out of the walls. The road was drying now, but everywhere the evidence showed that before spring had come the roads had been veritable morasses, impassable except by the bold and the strong.

There was no liverybarn yet. A horsetrader named Brice Fennelly was erecting one, but he had about all the trade he could accommodate without hiring out rigs and animals as it was.

It was Brice Fennelly who gave Reuben, Eulalia, and Little Bob Tollman their introduction to Newton. Fennelly was an Arkansas-boy. Arkansas and Kentucky weren't exactly side by side, but the section was the same; at least the sectionalism had been, lacking four

16

days of four full years of civil insurrection. That was all long past now, although folks still remembered, and when they met like this in a new world, a different environment, they had a kind of kinship to rely upon.

Brice was a bean-pole man with a long-jawed, thin face, topped by a mane of unkempt wild hair. He was one of those horsetraders who persevered in projecting the illusion of bumpkin stupidity. It worked so well Brice Fennelly now owned, aside from his corrals and half-built barn, seven business lots on Newton's main road, and a nice slice of creek-bottom land two miles north of town, out where the good-soil farming land was.

He pointed out the two saloons, one still with its tent-top, the other made of hewn logs so green the sap was running yet. And the freight yard across from the emporium; the barber shop with its candy-striped pole, the laundry shack pushed perilously between two large and taller buildings, even a stage office—next to the blacksmith's shop, which was itself beside a harness and saddle establishment.

"We're a-growin'," Fennelly said. "We're a-fixin' to have a right prosperous year again, too, folks. Newton'll someday be the capital o' Montana Territory, or I'm sure guessin' wrong. Look aroun' you, folks; look at that land out there; it's thigh-deep to hardpan. A man could bury a plow out there, sew in a crop o' spuds that wouldn't quit, or scratch over the top an' harrow-plant some rye or wheat or barley. Y'see that grass—how tall it is? To a knowin' man that's all the proof he'd need. Where grass grows like that, friends, the soil's rich, the land's deep-down. A hundred an' sixty acres around here'll make you independent for life."

Little Bob gazed at Brice Fennelly. "Were you a

farmer or trader back home?" he asked, and Brice scratched the tip of his long, droopy nose, obviously balancing between a lie and the truth. He sighed; the truth won out.

"I never farmed much, friend. Been a trader most of my days. But that don't mean I ain't on to real land when I see it." He waved out there where a golden morning sun was burnishing the land to a dull sheen. "I'm not tryin' to sell it, friends; I'm only pointin' out to you what I see in it." He dropped his hand, looked far out with a softness to his otherwise sharp, shrewd eyes, and said, "Hitch up, folks; drive out a ways. Run your hand into the ground, chew the stalks of that grass, feel the warmth of the air, then come back an' tell me I don't know what I'm talkin' about."

Little Bob said he'd like to see some worthwhile horses. Fennelly took them back to his corrals, behind where the barn was being erected. He sized up Little Bob, screwed up his face and sized up some horses in the first big corral. There wasn't a horsetrader worth his salt who didn't match a buyer to a horse. All that talk of traders slyly besting folks was largely hogwash. Sure enough—when a smart-alec came along, traders would sit up nights hatching ways to get his money, get him bucked off or run-away with, but all the tricks they knew were used almost exclusively for those types. Because a good deal of their business was repeat-trade, especially if they figured to stay in one place a few years, goodwill was important. But besides that, horsetraders were businessmen, not thieves. Like Brice Fennelly, who sized Little Bob up as a man who'd care for his beast, and selected a spotted-rump gelding with a ratty little tail and a wispy mane. Neither Bob nor Reuben had ever before seen such an oddly-marked horse.

"Appaloosie," stated Fennelly, with a frontiersman's disdain of correct pronunciation. "They come from down in Idaho an' Oregon. In'juns breed 'em. When they're yearlings they set 'em loose in a big race. The first ten winners they keep for stud, all the others are gelded. A lot of the oldtimers whose topknots depended on good horses, rode 'em. Tell you, friend; saddle him up and ride him out a ways. A man never got to know a horse from the ground."

Little Bob did exactly that. While he was gone Reuben and Eulalia walked up through Newton, occasionally being squeezed almost off the boardwalk by the push and press of strident, hurrying people. It was the first town of any importance they'd seen in a long time, except perhaps the down-river Missouri towns which they'd only passed through. They paused longest where a land merchant had his office. Here, painstakingly spelled out in an elaborate Spenserian hand, were land listings and descriptions one right after another. There was even homesteading information to be acquired inside, for just one dollar.

Reuben took his wife's arm to steer her inside. Several cowboys were coming down from the opposite direction, their faces tanned to a very dark color, their bodies loose and confident, their faces arrogant, a trifle scornful, the way it always was between the men who rode on top of horses and the men who walked behind them. When they were abreast of the land office they slowed to gaze at the little clutch of people standing outside reading the placards. One of them said in a half-laughing, half-serious Texas drawl, "Now you folks don' want to go takin' up land hereabouts. Cowmen been usin' this land a long time; they been buryin' redskins under it to fertilize the grass—but it's gettin' a

19

mite hard findin' redskins any more." The Texan paused, leered with obvious meaning, then rejoined his broadly smiling companions as they began walking along again. "Scrawny settlers wouldn't fertilize the grass as good anyhow," he said, then the three of them moved off laughing, their tied-down belt-guns swinging with each step.

Eulalia held tightly to big Reuben's hand. He watched those three for a moment from the doorway, turned finally and went on inside where three men with derby hats, sleeve-garters and poisonous cigars were as busy with land-hungry emigrants as three cats in the same box of shavings. Conversation was a constant drone of noise. As rapidly as one stool was vacated another emigrant sat upon it. The land was divided into parcels; there was excellent farm land at a stiff price, near-worthless land at a cheaper price. The highest-priced parcels had surface water on them—springs which ran year round. These were the pieces Reuben wanted to see.

It took a long time, partly because there were so many parcels up for grabs, partly because big Reuben was cautious and methodical about this; it was, after all, what he'd come more than a thousand miles to find, and all the painful days and nights were pitted against a couple of noisy, frenzied hours, now, in a tent-town land office. The wrong decision at this point could mean everything else had gone for nothing.

When he and Eulalia left, they had four slips of paper with them, plus the warning of the land-clerk back there not to delay too long because every day other folks were staking out claims, too. A man who procrastinated usually found someone else starting his house and fences on the same land.

20

They strolled back down to their camp. Little Bob was already there sitting in the shade of the old wagon gazing with prideful admiration at a spotted-rump horse grazing yonder with the other animals. Reuben eyed the horse for a quiet moment, then smiled. Eulalia asked Little Bob how he was under saddle, and as was his custom, Little Bob said only: "He'll do."

They left Eulalia at their camp the following morning and rode out, Bob on his spotted-rump horse, to look at the land. Three of the parcels lay westerly. One lay up north of town. It adjoined the larger parcel already owned by Brice Fennelly, but they didn't discover that until they came upon a sign stating that the land marked out was not for sale or trade, giving Fennelly's name as owner.

The northward piece was best; it had a tributary of the creek which ran out back of town, through it nearly the full length. The land wasn't entirely level, but neither was it too tilted for plowing and harvesting. In a rocky corner of the place there was a wood-lot of second-growth pines and firs, and up there, too, they came upon a number of sunken circles in the ground they were puzzled by until Little Bob dismounted, kicked around, and turned up a place where refuse had been thrown. There, they found broken obsidian arrowpoints and the flaky chips where more arrowpoints had been made. The sunken circles, evidently, were tipi-rings; places where the earth had been packed down through a long series of winters by moccasined feet. This had been an Indian campground in years past.

They were still in the wood-lot when Bob's horse threw up its head, catching their attention as it peered off westerly. Two riders were loping forward, easy in their saddles as only bred-horsemen ever were. Bob and

Reuben stood back in the trees watching. But those men out there were as hawk-eyed as Indians; they passed no ambushing sites without habitually making a careful survey. They saw the Tollmans watching, and slowed to a steady walk, squinting over into the trees as they came on.

For a while it seemed they'd skirt far out and around, but in the end they altered course and came right on up. Reuben and Bob went ahead a few yards, realizing the newcomers had seen them and were coming over. They studied the rangemen with cautious interest and when those two drew rein and returned this look of careful curiosity, big Reuben said it was a good morning for riding out. The cowboys nodded about that, still quietly studious, then the older one, a man in his lean, tough forties who hadn't shaved for several days, said, "You fellers lookin' over the land?"

Reuben said that they were; that they were Kentuckians come out to the frontier for a fresh start. The cowboys digested this calmly, then the older one said, "Well, boys; she's a good country, except she's gettin' almighty cluttered up these past few years." He switched his attention to Bob and the spotted-rump horse. "Figured you might be thievin' Crows or Blackfeet when we seen that horse," he said, and drew up his thin-lipped mouth a little. "Figured we might have a little fun; then we seen you was white men." He looked over at his stony-faced, silent companion. "Jute; trade the feller out of his speckled horse. You're always sayin' you want one of 'em."

The man called Jute wasn't more than twenty-two or twenty-three, but his face was scarred with little lines up around his steady, shrewd eyes. He shrugged, gauging Bob and big Reuben. "Fellers as big as these two," he

22

murmured, "could plow up the land with nothin' more between 'em than a stout set o' chain-harness." It was meant as a rough joke. Jute smiled. So did the other rangerider. "You care to dicker on that horse?" Jute asked. Bob shook his head without speaking. There was something about those two that jangled on his nerves. It wasn't their talk or even their expressions; it was something that went deeper; something he felt strongly but couldn't define, even to himself.

Jute studied the horse a moment longer then lifted his rein-hand. "Didn't hardly figure you would, mister," he said. "I don't allow he'd be any bettern' any other horse. It's just that I've never owned one an' sort of figure I'd like to try one some time."

Reuben said, "You fellers from around here?"

The older man raised an arm, pointing westerly. "From Cromwell's outfit," he said casually, as though everyone knew the Cromwell outfit. "Got a cow-camp about three miles yonder." He dropped the arm, gazed a moment at Reuben, then said, "We try'n keep the cattle from driftin' over this way an' eatin' up the garden patches these settlers set out every spring. But it's gettin' harder to do every year; settlers keep fannin' out farther to the west. 'Course; most of 'em only last a year or two. But it's still a headache, keepin' the cattle away."

"Why?" Reuben asked. "Why do they only last a year or two?"

Jute said, near to smiling at Reuben, "Mister; a hundred an' sixty acres in this country isn't near enough for a man to make a livin' on. If he farms, he's got to eat all his own produce 'cause all the other settlers is doin' the same thing an' there's just no market for all the stuff they raise. If he tries his hand with cattle, a hundred an'

23

sixty, 'specially durin' a dry year, isn't enough land for more'n a couple o' milk cows. Still; they keep comin'; they keep tryin'."

Reuben turned silent, and Little Bob, who hadn't spoken at all, continued to study their visitors. Eventually, the cowboys whirled and rode off, loping on over the golden springtime land with the Tollman brothers watching them until they were small in the burnished distance.

As they were mounting up Bob said, "Rube; we'd better do some askin' around. Fennelly'd know whether what those fellers said was the truth or not."

They didn't look over the parcel of land after that, but instead set their horses back towards town. Over near the stageroad they encountered a train of four immense freight wagons grinding their way down towards Newton at a snail's pace, partly drawn by horses, partly by sleek mules. Farther along they met a coach rocking on its leather springs as it raced past, northward-bound. Then they picked up the din and clangor of Newton itself, a fiercely busy town thriving on the emigrant trade.

They didn't try bucking the roadway traffic, but rode out and around, and came into the back-lot of Fennelly's trading compound, where three carpenters were profanely at work on the barn.

CHAPTER FOUR

THEY LEFT BRICE FENNELLY AHEAD OF DUSK AND rode silently back to camp where Eulalia had supper simmering. She'd had callers today, she told them, as they off-saddled near the fire. Another emigrant woman

24

who was camped farther up the creek, and her ten-year-old pigtailed daughter. "From Tennessee, Reuben. Her husband came home from the war with a crippled arm."

Little Bob took the horses out to grass and was a long time strolling back to eat. He used swatches of bent grass to scrub the salt-sweat off his animal's back.

Reuben was explaining to Eulalia what Brice Fennelly had told them when Little Bob returned, sank down upon a block of wood and accepted his tin plate of stew from Eulalia.

"The cowboys were right, Eulalia, we've got to have more'n just the hundred and sixty acres."

"But Mister Fennelly said a man could become independent for life on—"

"I realize what he said," muttered big Reuben. "And he didn't deliberately try to mislead us. But then, Bob and I had a long talk with him this evenin'. He's no farmer; never has been a farmer. He was repeatin' what other folks said."

Eulalia looked around where Little Bob was tucked up, calmly eating his supper. She looked back at her husband, anxious and troubled. "But; what will we do now?" she asked.

"I'll take up a hundred and sixty too," said Little Bob quietly. "We already went back'n paid the entrance fee at the land office for the parcel adjoinin' the other piece."

Eulalia looked at her husband when Little Bob went back to eating. "You filed on a piece?" she said a little breathlessly. He nodded, smiling at her with his eyes.

"A little creek runs through it. There's a wood-lot for the cabin and outbuildings. Tomorrow we'll drive out and set up our last camp, Eulalia."

She settled back on her wooden stool with mixed feelings. She gazed at the purple skies; after all the
25

wandering and anguish—the loss of little Jonas—she was home again. It would require some getting used to. She gazed over where Bob sat, thinking back to what he'd told her the night before. They'd been wanderers so long it seemed somehow unreal, the prospect of settling down in one place.

"With Bob's land we'll have over three hundred good acres. With Fennelly's piece we'll have—"

"Fennelly's piece, Reuben; did you buy more land?"

"Leased it from him for one year with the right to buy at the end of that time if we calculate we need it."

She was silent; this was all very sudden. Also, it was a little frightening. From one hundred and sixty acres, they'd now have three hundred and twenty deeded, and another three hundred and twenty leased. It was more than a square mile. While that was a breathtakingly large farm back in Kentucky, she'd soon enough learn it wasn't much of a ranch in Montana Territory, where cattlemen figured their holdings in sections of land. Each section was one square mile.

"Bob . . . ?" she said quietly.

He had put aside the empty plate and was holding the tin cup of coffee cradled in both his large hands, gazing down the pleasant night. He turned, showed her his unsmiling face, and gently inclined his head at her. "I told you," he murmured. "Out here we'll either stand or fall, an' it'll be entirely up to us, Eulalia."

They discussed their acquisition for another hour then retired. For Eulalia it took a lot of getting used to. Day before yesterday they'd been what they'd always been; at least what they'd always *seemed* to be, dispossessed wanderers creaking and bumping their way across an endlessly changing land, every mile of it foreign to them. For a year and longer they'd been on the road. All

26

of a sudden all that had abruptly ended. She went to sleep fiercely praying into her pillow, and the following morning when the men were up and stirring, her husband showing a freshness to his way of moving, her brother-in-law still unsmiling, but sometimes humming the snatch of some old marching song, she couldn't help but pray again. Not for herself, but for them. They were good men; but life was indifferent to a man's quality, mostly; it seemed only concerned with his activity.

They struck camp, loaded up, moved out cutting wide around Newton and heading northward with Little Bob on his spotted-rump horse riding scout on ahead, his shotgun, as always, teetering across the saddle-seat, in the warm and fragrant Montana morning.

They reached their land just as a pair of riders came in off the eastward stageroad towards it, too. Little Bob rode over to those men and shortly afterwards returned to say the strangers had been looking for land. He'd explained this piece was spoken for. The strangers had then ridden off northward to search some more.

They set up camp near the little creek. For the first time in more than a year, the men worked without simply going through motions; Bob snaked in two dead-falls to their camp for firewood. Reuben set out their grinding wheel and sat hunched, his right leg rhythmically pumping as he honed their axes. He rummaged through the tools for their saws, and assembled them. There was very little said between the three of them. Eulalia did as she always did in camp; she stacked wood near the fire-ring, set up the tripod for their iron kettles, aired their ticking quilts, organized their daily lives at the camp, then her share was finished except for the thrice-daily chore of cooking, the weekly chore of beating soiled clothing

27

upon the creek-side stones, the planning and managing.

For four days Reuben and Little Bob worked hard at plumbing and squaring the fir-log foundation for a cabin and a barn. For seven days after that they felled timber at the northerly wood-lot and adzed the logs to size after skidding them to the building site.

Each day they came into camp sore and bruised and pleasantly tired. Reuben often took her walking in the soft evenings; they'd kneel and feel the soil, or they'd go up the little creek looking for a high enough place to make their dam, so that the gravity fall would give her plenty of water pressure at the house.

And scarcely without any of them noticing it, spring turned into summer, the heat came, curing grass on the stem, their animals got fat again, and spent the days when they weren't needed up in the wood-lot swishing their tails at the endless droves of deer-flies, small, fiercely competitive little nuisances that stung when they bit.

Brice Fennelly rode out once and drove out once. Trying new horses, he told them, but his shrewd eyes missed nothing and he seemed pleased at their progress. The last time he was out he told Eulalia, sounding pleased with himself, that judging horseflesh was second-nature to him; he'd been doing it all his life. But judging men was a hobby, and he wasn't as confident in himself in this field. His long, homely face had brightened, his hard, calculating eyes smiled, and he said, "But I'm about ready to say I'm gettin' on at it, Miz Tollman. I sure done m'self proud on them two. Not only are they big as all outdoors an' strong t'match, but they're hones' men, true to what they tell a man, an' believe me, *that's* right hard to come by any more in men."

They were roofing the cabin when the same pair of cowboys rode over one afternoon that Bob and Reuben had met their first trip to the land. The one called Jute rode all around the house, studying it. His older, unshaven companion got down and accepted a dipper of water from Eulalia. Then he gazed at her with strong admiration, saying almost wistfully that it'd been a long time since he'd stood and visited a spell with a right handsome woman.

Reuben climbed down to visit with those two, but not Little Bob; he worked on, giving the pair of rangemen only a grave nod.

Three days later a band of cattle ambled over nearby and grazed off a patch of good grass before Eulalia heard them and walked out a ways to see. Afterwards, Little Bob saddled his spotted-rump horse and drove them off. The fourth day they were back again, only more of them this time, so Little Bob drove them farther, and came upon the cow-camp of the pair of Cromwell cowboys. Neither rider was at the camp. They had a lariat strung between two trees for drying clothes. There was a little rickety pole-corral with one corner of it across a muddy place where a spring trickled up out of the ground. Their bedrolls were carelessly lying there, and they had their provisions in a wooden box which they pulled up into the lower branches of a pine, to keep rodents and larger animals from stealing them blind.

He considered leaving a note about the cattle but didn't, and had ridden about a mile back towards home when two men intercepted him, riding down from the north. One of them was a dark, swarthy cowboy with an ivory-handled sixgun. He looked rough and capable. He nodded at Little Bob but didn't say a word. The other

29

man was large, heavy, grey around the temples and was riding a handsome chestnut horse. This man had the look and manners of someone other than a hired hand. Even before he identified himself as Benton Cromwell, Little Bob had guessed who he was.

He told Cromwell and the black-eyed, harsh-faced man he'd just drifted some cattle back on to the cow-camp range. Benton Cromwell kept eyeing Bob all the while, nodding his head at what the younger man was saying, but leaving Bob with the impression his thoughts weren't on the cattle at all.

Finally Cromwell said, "I've seen the cabin you folks're putting up. They tell me you've got a barn laid out too." He said these things in a dry, inflectionless voice, still making his private appraisal of Little Bob. "You know; you folks aren't the first who've staked that land. The others never proved up. Lasted a year, didn't they, Ned?"

The swarthy man nodded, still studying Little Bob, still keeping slightly in the background, silent all the while.

"They couldn't make it, Mister Tollman," said Cromwell. "It's a hard life, out here, on a hundred and sixty acres."

Bob caught the implication behind Cromwell's words. He said quietly, "Maybe we won't either. But we sure aim to try."

Cromwell nodded again, in the same assessing way. "Sure," he murmured. "A man's got to try, hasn't he?"

"Yes."

"Well; good luck, Mister Tollman. If the cattle bother you, let me know. I'll have someone fetch them back."

Little Bob resumed his way homeward weighing and balancing Benton Cromwell, sifting through the exterior to reach what was behind it, and coming to no definite conclusion. With a powerful and successful man such as Benton Cromwell obviously was, you couldn't guess it all the first time around. But one thing seemed certain; Cromwell wasn't a man to make enemies until he was good and ready to do so. But on the other hand there wasn't much doubt about something else: If Benton Cromwell decided a man was his enemy, he'd work just as hard at being unfriendly as most men worked at making friends.

Little Bob related at supper that evening his encounter over near the cow-camp. He also said he didn't expect the cattle to stay away; that whether Jute and his pardner were supposed to be on the job or not, the fact was, they weren't on the job, and that meant, simply, that Cromwell's critters would keep coming back.

Eulalia smoothed that over by saying that since they had only their four horses, at least now, the grass might as well be used by Cromwell's cattle.

Reuben was quiet about that, although he murmured something about picking up a few head when they were set up to handle them, and for that reason he'd just as soon their grass wasn't cropped off.

Little Bob was right. Three days later the same bunch of critters were back again. The fourth day still more came drifting down from the north. Little Bob rode out that afternoon to push them back, he said, but he did more than that; he back-tracked until he found what he'd thought might be out there—shod-horse tracks. Those cattle hadn't just wandered over, they'd been steered in the right direction by two men on horseback.

He returned home and said nothing beyond the fact that he'd pushed Cromwell's critters back over where they belonged. But Reuben came around after Eulalia

31

was abed; Reuben knew his younger brother; knew the steady, cold look in his eye when he saw it. He drew up one of their homemade chairs, eased down beside Little Bob's wall bunk, and said, "They have a little help, getting down here, Bob?"

From his stretched-out position Little Bob looked over and nodded. "A little. Two mounted men. I reckon they'd be Jute and the other one—the feller who only shaves every couple weeks."

"Well," mused big Reuben in his quiet way, "you reckon that's why the other folks never were able to make it out here?"

"I did have some such thought," murmured Little Bob, settling his head upon both upraised arms. "It'd be a good way to keep folks from infringin' on his range. I don't know that's so, at all, but I'd like to hear from Fennelly why the others pulled out."

Reuben thought a while, then said, "Cromwell strike you as a reasoning man, Bob?"

The younger brother chose his words carefully, for if Reuben knew his younger brother, Little Bob also knew Reuben. "A reasonin' man—yes. But only if the reasonin' went all his way, Rube. He's smooth an' polite, an' he looks down inside a man takin' his measure all the time he's talkin' to him. I'd just guess that if you go reasonin' with Cromwell, Rube, he's goin' to agree with you one hundred per cent. But we'll keep right on gettin' his critters over here eatin' down our grass."

Reuben went to bed and Little Bob lay a long while with his arms propping up his head, turning things over in his mind. What he particularly recalled was the way Cromwell had told him the others had failed on this same claim. It wasn't the statement he remembered, it

32

was the dry, expectant way it had been made.

He also recalled that black-eyed, swarthy man riding with Cromwell. He'd seen plenty of that kind before.

CHAPTER FIVE

THEY FINISHED THE CABIN IN THE GROWING HEAT. They completed the barn with a lemon-yellow sun up there malevolently hazing the cowed countryside. After that, they hauled cedar posts from the brakes fifteen miles east of Newton, and built their corrals. They were berry-brown and hard as stone from those labors. They had their lives and their land organized, but they had no cattle yet, and in fact practical Reuben said, since it was getting along towards fall, he thought they should wait until about the following March to buy any.

"Work out in the meantime?" asked Bob.

"That," agreed Reuben, "or hunt. Either way it'll bring in the vittals we'll need through the cold months. Hunt, and rack up some cord-wood."

They hunted far and wide. They found the headquarters of the Cromwell outfit, they got to be familiar with the land on all sides of their claim. They even spent three days one time packing into the far-away hills for upland grouse and, with luck, some bear-meat. They didn't get the bear-meat but they came back with a nice bunch of blue grouse. Reuben told Eulalia he was just as satisfied they didn't get a bear anyway.

"No acorns back in those hills. Too wet a spring I reckon. Anyway, when a bear dens-up he fills up on acorns. When there aren't any, he fills upon scavenge. The meat smells rotten when it's bein' cooked. It'll smell up a whole house."

33

They cut wood up at the wood-lot, hauled it down and tiered it out back, convenient for Eulalia. They also turned back Cromwell's cattle from time to time and once, when they encountered Jute and his whiskery pardner, whose name was Texas Harkins, Reuben said maybe it'd help if they put up some kind of a fence, but Texas Harkins sadly shook his head.

"They're breachy," he said, referring to the cattle. "Once cattle learn how to lean and get their heads through, isn't hardly a fence in the country'd keep 'em out. 'Course; you boys can suit yourselves about that fence. Alls I'm sayin' is once critters get breachy, they'll breach any fence folks put up."

After they'd ridden off Little Bob, who'd remained silent all through the little visit back there, quietly said Cromwell's range critters were too wild to be breachy, and that furthermore if they came through a man's fence, they'd have a little two-legged help at it.

There was a little whip in the air; a little crackle to the earth in the grey mornings when Little Bob and Reuben went out to chuck hay to their corralled horses. Bob's spotted-rump horse grew hair like a goat. Eulalia laughed, saying he looked like a bear or a sheep.

They brought her back seven laying hens and a big rooster from town one day, and she was so occupied with making straw nests and roosts in a closed-off corner of the big log barn she was late with their supper.

Autumn brought changes. In Kentucky there were many years when there was no autumn at all; just summer and winter. But Montana had four definite seasons, and fall wasn't the least bit bashful about announcing itself. It seemed to come right after midnight about two weeks after they'd fetched home those chickens. It awoke them whistling over the roof-ridge and scrabbling beneath the overhang-eaves. It winnowed its way through the cracks and plummeted the temperature to zero in a matter of a very few hours. Little Bob got up and padded out back to fetch in a couple of chunks of wood to heave into their pot-bellied iron stove, but something delayed him after he opened the rear door and looked out where a crooked old pewter moon, riding the bucking clouds, cast its steely brightness downward over the wind-whipped world. There was a horseman sitting out there maybe fifty yards beyond the corner of the barn.

He wasn't doing anything, just sitting on his horse out there hunched up inside a heavy sheepskin rider's coat, gazing down at the house. Little Bob moved back, eased the door nearly closed, and watched. For about ten minutes that man lingered out there, not moving. His horse had its head down, its tail tucked against the piercing wind. Finally, the rider turned and slowly rode off westerly. Once, when the wind dropped, Little Bob thought he heard two riders. But the only one he saw was that man in the sheepskin coat.

He got the chunks of fir, put them in the stove, then got dressed, buckled on his sixgun, shrugged into his heavy coat, picked up his shotgun and went outside. For a while he stood motionless against the rear log wall of the house, looking and listening. Then he went across to the barn and stepped inside, waited again for something to snag his attention, and when nothing did, he began an inspection. For a half-hour he went back and forth, but he found nothing missing, or moved, or out of place, which didn't make much sense. He considered climbing to the loft where he and Reuben had pitched up their hay, but he didn't, and in the end, wide awake and chilled through by the biting cold, he strolled out back to gaze

35

off into the westerly night. It was as still and empty out there as though the whole thing had been an illusion.

He returned to the house, shucked his armament and clothing, checked the stove, then crawled back into this bunk, puzzled and mystified. He'd seen the mounted man all right; that was no illusion, but maybe he'd been only a camp-robber looking for something worthwhile to steal. Perhaps there'd been a pair of them; he believed he'd heard two horses when the visible one had turned to ride off. It was possible, providing the second man had kept the barn between himself and the house, which would have prevented anyone at the house from seeing him.

There was a way to make certain. As soon as daylight came, grey and cold and dismal, Little Bob got dressed and went down to the barn for the choring. He fed the animals, then he made a careful study of the ground inside and outside. There *had* been two of them. One had been inside the barn, the other one had evidently been the sentry. Moreover, they wore the boots of cowmen.

He didn't mention any of this to Reuben or Eulalia, but later on when Reuben suggested going into town to buy a set of traps at the general store, Bob found an excuse for staying home. He wanted to sharpen their axes and grease the harness.

But it was a wasted day. He did the things he'd said he had to do, and all the time he kept studying the grey land beneath its leaden, scudding old clouds, but it remained as empty as it usually was. He did see some Cromwell cattle to the north, picking in the protected swales, but that was all.

Reuben returned without any traps. Brice Fennelly had told him buying traps would be a waste of money;

36

the fur-bearing critters had been all but trapped into extinction years before, unless they wanted to go a hundred miles north up into the high mountains, and if they did that there was an excellent chance they'd be snowed in up there and unable to return home until the springtime thaws arrived.

In the darkening afternoon Little Bob saddled his horse and drove the Cromwell cattle back over on to their land. It was no longer important, saving the grass, but that wasn't the point now; Cromwell's cattle had become a source of annoyance. When they appeared, Little Bob just naturally went out to push them back where they belonged.

A week after those nocturnal visitors Ned Bowman, Cromwell's swarthy, taciturn rangeboss rode into the yard to ask if either Reuben or Bob had seen a band of loose horses wearing Cromwell's big rib-brand: BC? They told him they hadn't and because it was bitterly cold out Reuben invited Bowman in for a cup of broth. The rangeboss declined, looked around the yard, then rode off northwesterly. Reuben caught Little Bob watching; he knew that still, alert expression and said, "What's the matter?"

"Just wonderin'," murmured Little Bob, and went ambling down to the barn.

It was two days after Ned Bowman's visit that Little Bob went riding northward to test a notion he had. There was no plausible explanation for those nocturnal visitors, but he had an idea that by this time Cromwell's men would have an established routine about the cattle. They'd been at it long enough—since early spring—to have a pattern they'd follow.

He went around the shoulder of a low hill, left his horse in some trees on the far side, climbed to the top

37

and lay up there with the increasing cold coming down out of the late-day north turning the dead grass brittle with hoar-frost.

It was an uncomfortable wait. He beat his hands together and once he swung his arms, but eventually they came, two of them, drifting a little band of critters ahead of them, coated and gauntleted against the cold, riding as though they wanted to get this over with and get back to a warm bunkhouse.

He let them pass down-country for a half mile before going back to his animal, mounting up and riding down behind them with his scattergun across his lap, his belt-gun beneath his sheepskin coat.

It got dark early. In fact, by three-thirty in the afternoon visibility was cut in half. By four o'clock it was dusk. He was able to keep the men and the cattle in sight as far as the Tollman property line, which was as far as he had go anyway, to be sure what they were up to, so after that he jogged right on up behind them, split out when they went westerly around a landswell, passing around the same swell easterly, and when they halted on the far side he lay his scattergun across the forearm of his rein-hand, cocked one barrel and walked his horse up to within a hundred feet of them before they heard him and swung around.

Jute and Texas Harkins. He wasn't surprised at that. He rode on up another fifty feet, halted and dropped his reins. They were armed; each had a Winchester saddle gun under his right leg, and beneath their coats, buttoned up to the throat against the cold, each man also had a sixgun. But they might as well have left their weapons back at the BC bunkhouse for all the good they'd do them now.

Little Bob lowered the shotgun, let it balance upon

38

the horn of his saddle. He said nothing and neither did the other two. Harkins was fresh-shaved, for a change. His thin face was pale where the beard-stubble had been. Sturdy Jute Daily had a woollen scarf wrapped around his throat. They both wore chaps. This time of year they weren't worn to protect the legs from thorny brush, but as a shield against the bitter cold.

"Just tell me one thing," Little Bob said, "is this the way Cromwell drove off the other settlers?"

Jute flicked a look to Harkins and the Texan ignored it. He kept eyeing Bob Tollman. There was a way to loosen a man's tongue under these circumstances and Little Bob employed it. He cocked the other barrel of his scattergun. At fifty feet that thing would make mincemeat out of a man. He shifted the ugly barrels a little bringing them to bear upon Texas Harkin's chest.

"Never did believe in a lot of unnecessary talk," murmured Little Bob. "One thing about a shotgun; without makin' any noise it's got a right eloquent way of makin' its point. You got five seconds to answer, Mister Harkins."

"All I know is what I'm told to do," the Texan said. "I'm only a hired rider."

Bob eased off one of the hammers. It wasn't a direct answer but it was good enough. "Ride around 'em," he said, "an' take 'em straight back the way you drove 'em down here."

Jute lifted his reins and sighed. He and Texas Harkins started riding stiffly out and around. Little Bob moved well away. His shotgun was useless at carbine range; those two had carbines. He didn't believe they'd try anything, but taking foolish chances wasn't a weakness of his.

39

It was dark long before Jute and Texas Harkins got the drifting cattle headed back towards Cromwell range again, but despite this, Little Bob could tell by the noise that he was being obeyed.

Later, he went home, put up his horse, crossed over to the house and stepped inside into a warm blaze of orange lamplight. He put aside his scattergun and coat. Eulalia set out his supper and Reuben came in from another room to lean in the doorway. Neither he nor his wife said a word. They didn't have to, actually; Little Bob's tight, cold expression told them something had happened.

Eulalia poured a second cup of coffee and big Reuben ambled on over, dropped down opposite his brother and warmed his hands around the cup, waiting. Little Bob took the edge off his hunger first, then he told them what he'd done. They had a scarred old Seth Thomas clock they'd brought all the way from Kentucky with them. It stood upon a kitchen shelf making its steady unruffled sound, imperturbable, untouched by all it had survived in the past hundred years, and, at least to Eulalia, provided a cadenced kind of solid comfort, solid reassurance.

"Well," Reuben murmured, after a while, "the cattle really couldn't damage us much this time of year."

Little Bob nodded in solemn agreement. "That's right," he agreed, and drank coffee before saying more. "I reckon though, it's not the cattle—nor the time of year, Rube. They'll be back again come new grass. It's a simple thing the way they do it. No guns, no fights, no hard words; you just wear folks down. You let the cattle do it for you. They eat another man's graze and destroy his garden patch an' fret him day'n night all year round."

40

"I figured we'd fence in the spring, Bob."

"Sure," mumbled the younger man, and dropped his head so they wouldn't see his face. "You heard 'em, Rube. They weren't complaining about their cattle the time they told us the critters were breachy. I didn't think they were doing so at the time." He raised his eyes to his brother. "They were warning us; they as good as told us not to build fences because they'd push the cattle right through 'em."

The clock ticked and Eulalia got them more coffee; Bob finished his supper and big Reuben sat back, drumming atop the plank-top table. "We can't leave," said Reuben in a low voice. "Everything we've got is sunk into the ground right here. We can't move again."

Little Bob avoided his sister-in-law's eyes and said, "I don't reckon that we ought to."

Reuben stopped the drumming. "I'll ride over and reason with him," he stated, meaning he'd try and talk to Benton Cromwell.

Bob nodded, looked rueful. "Sure," he murmured. "Take along your scattergun."

Eulalia stood with her back to the stove, both hands clenched in front of her stomach, looking at the pair of big men. It was the custom where they'd come from to call the youngest son "Little" meaning younger, and back there no one saw anything odd about a man who weighed a hundred and eighty-five pounds and who stood six feet and two inches, being called "Little" Bob; it only meant he had an older brother.

But tonight for the first time, it struck Eulalia as an incongruous thing: there he sat with his glass-clear eyes and his long-lipped mouth, his high cheekbones and his quiet violence, talking gentle and looking deadly. They weren't very much alike, those two, she thought, but

41

they were Kentuckians, and kinship was an exalted thing among Kentuckians. It was difficult to understand, and she loved her husband very much, but there was no escaping it; Reuben had no stomach for violence and Little Bob seemed to have gotten his own share and Reuben's share as well, of unyielding hardness.

"It's late," she softly told them. "It's best we went to bed. In the morning things'll look different."

Little Bob stood up, gazing at her, his eyes sardonic. "Yeah," he told her quietly. "It'll be daylight an' right now it's dark. That's the only difference we'll see. Good night."

CHAPTER SIX

FOR THREE DAYS THEY STUCK CLOSE, AND ALTHOUGH they found plenty to do—there was always plenty to do—and talked about the little details of their existence in the grey, raw prairie world, each of them from time to time scanned the northward plains and the westerly prairie.

But no more cattle drifted down to annoy them. Eulalia said one evening Mister Cromwell probably felt chagrined; he wouldn't send the critters down any more. Reuben muttered a kind of guarded assent to that and Little Bob, cleaning guns over by their pot-bellied iron stove, went right on, as though no one had spoken.

The fourth day Ned Bowman rode in from the eastward stageroad wearing a sheepskin coat and heavy gauntlets. He stopped out in the yard as he always did, looking around.

He'd been drinking; his eyes were very bright and his

cheeks were unnaturally red. But what really told Reuben and Bob that Ned was carrying a load was his talk. Normally Bowman said exactly what he had to say in as few words as possible. Today he rambled. He said, looking straight down from the saddle at Little Bob, "Quite a tracker, ain't you, emigrant. 'Course, this time o' year slippin' up behind folks with a shotgun's not so hard, because it gets dark early. Still; you done it right clever—so I was told."

Reuben said, "Come inside, Ned, and have a cup of coffee." He could feel trouble coming and he was a reasoning man who'd avoid it every time that he could.

"No coffee," growled Bowman, throwing a contemptuous look at big Reuben. "I don't go inside emigrant shacks, mister, any more'n I go inside stinkin' Injun tipis." Ned turned back to Little Bob again. "There's such a thing as bein' too damned smart," he said. "You know what I mean?"

Little Bob was leaning with both arms hooked over the tie-rack out front of the barn. He didn't answer; he didn't even move his head, but the look was there in his crystal eyes.

"Cat got your tongue?" Bowman demanded. "Too scairt to answer? All right, emigrant; that suits me fine, only just remember what I told you about gettin' too big for your britches." Bowman reined his horse around and went out of the yard with Little Bob standing there gazing after him.

Reuben thought it'd be a fine idea for them to hitch up the following morning and ride into Newton. Eulalia, he said, needed the outing, and besides that, it would do them all good to have a change of scenery for a little while.

Nothing more was said about Ned Bowman's visit.

43

When Eulalia asked them what Cromwell's rangeboss had wanted, Little Bob had strolled on through the kitchen to tend the stove and Reuben had lingered out there with his wife to say something about Bowman passing through on his way home from town.

They drove into town the next morning, all three of them on the wagon-seat bundled against the cold, and when they hauled up out back of Brice Fennelly's new liverybarn Brice came out to lend Eulalia a hand down, then he sent her into the office where he had a stove and some coffee. He helped Reuben and Little Bob put up the team, fork them feed and heave the harness into the wagon. Then, when he started for the warm office also, Little Bob caught his arm.

" 'Like you to explain something to me," said the taller, younger man. " 'Like you to tell me why you never told us there'd been other folks settle that land out there."

Fennelly's glance jumped from big Reuben back to Little Bob. He said, "Well; what's the difference? You know how it is. You can see 'em all up an' down the land; some got the grit, some ain't. Some just naturally let—"

"It couldn't have been," spoke up Little Bob, "that you're scairt of Cromwell yourself, and keep givin' folks lease to that land o' yours in the hope that someday, someone'll come along who'll stand up to him."

Brice Fennelly rolled his eyes, saying, "Oh now wait a minute, Li'l Bob; you got this all wrong. I wouldn't put folks out there figurin' to get them into a fight with Benton Cromwell."

"But you knew he ran off the others, Brice. You had to know that."

"Well yes, I knew, but I just told you; some got grit an' some ain't."

"If you knew, why didn't you tell us?"

Fennelly was being driven to the wall and he knew it, evidently, because he looked over at big Reuben and said, "Hell, Rube; what's got into him to talk to me this-a-way? I done went out'n my way to see you folks got set up just right." Reuben didn't comment; he simply stood there gazing down at Brice. Fennelly gestured, he shot a look back and forth, he said, "Listen; we got a deputy U.S. marshal here now. Last year there wasn't no law. Let's go up an' talk to him about Benton Cromwell pickin' on you folks."

Little Bob shook his head. "If we need him," he told the liveryman coldly, "we'll come after him. What I wanted to get right in m'mind, Brice, was whether you were what I thought you might be, or not. Let's go, Rube."

They left Fennelly standing back down there in the center of his runway, gazing up after them. They got Eulalia and walked up town.

It was a cold day again, but for a change the sky was clear blue, and the sun was shining. It didn't cast a particle of heat downward, frost stood everywhere, there was no heat but at least there was a pleasant golden brightness which, after the monotonous days of greyness, was a genuine blessing.

A high-sided freight outfit was snug to the plankwalk over at the general store with two burly men unloading it. A number of idlers were watching. It was difficult to tell which of them were smoking and which weren't; all of them breathed clouds when they spoke, smoke, or steam from the cold.

They let Eulalia walk them over there to inspect the new bolt goods and against his better judgement Reuben

45

paid for three yards of blue gingham. Eulalia's eyes sparkled, her cheeks were as red as autumn apples. She smiled, pleased at being in Newton after the weeks alone at the claim. Reuben humored her, so did Little Bob, but in a different way. They ate at the restaurant with Little Bob paying, this time, then, as they were leaving, he paused in the doorway to gaze back. A very handsome girl across the room was watching him. He glanced straight back. She didn't lower her eyes nor act flustered at being caught staring. They looked until Eulalia brushed Little Bob's arm making a low, scandalized clucking sound, then he followed his brother and sister-in-law outside.

It wasn't a good moment for them to walk from the restaurant. Benton Cromwell and Ned Bowman were just turning in. Reuben stepped politely aside. Cromwell barged right past. So did Ned, but Bowman was more careless; he bumped Eulalia hard. Reuben was too far back but Little Bob wasn't; he was directly behind his sister-in-law and when Bowman started past Bob caught him by the coat-front, hauling Bowman up short.

"You bumped the lady," murmured Little Bob.

Bowman growled a curse and struck Bob's arm away. He took one step backward. "How do I know she's a lady?" he snarled, black eyes showing fire-points. "The next time you put a hand on me, emigrant, I'll break you in two. Get out of the way!"

Cromwell was crossing the restaurant towards that handsome girl across the room. He didn't know what was happening back by the door. The girl did though; she slowly came up to her feet, over there, still watching Little Bob, but with a totally different, frozen expression now.

Little Bob reached over, gently shoved Eulalia towards her husband, and said, "Bowman; I'm tellin' you she's a lady. An' if you want to go on an' get your dinner, you'd better apologize—once for bumpin' into her when you didn't have to—once for that remark you just made about her."

Cromwell's rangeboss already had his coat unbuttoned. Now, he swept the right-hand side of it back. That's as far as his hand got. Little Bob was less than two feet off; he swung without seeming to make any preparation to do so. The first took Bowman deep in the middle making Bowman's black eyes pop wide, making his lower jaw sag. The second strike was even harder. Little Bob was pivoting on his right foot throwing his weight behind that one. It doubled Bowman over.

Little Bob caught Bowman's coat and hustled the retching man over to the edge of the plankwalk, and heaved with both hands. Bowman fell out there in the dirt and jack-knifed clutching at his middle.

Benton Cromwell hurtled past Reuben and Eulalia. He stopped stiffly, looking at Ned Bowman. People came over to also stand at the edge of the plankwalk, staring in stunned silence. Ned Bowman was known as a fighting man as well as a rangeboss.

Little Bob turned to face Cromwell. "Mighty poor manners your foreman's got," he said quietly. "Where we come from, Mister Cromwell, a man makes a remark against a woman, we usually kill him."

Cromwell turned, several rangemen were coming up to join the crowd. He gestured to them. "Get Ned out of the road; take him over and put him in my buggy," he commanded, then he turned on Little Bob, his blue eyes turning icy. "That was a bad mistake," he said. "Ned

47

works for me, yes, but his private life, and his private feuds, are his own affair. Emigrant; he'll kill you."

The handsome girl was there, in the forefront of the crowd, as silent and staring as were the others. Little Bob saw her from the corner of his eye. He also saw the others, including his sister-in-law and his brother. They were shaken and chagrined. He regarded Benton Cromwell a moment longer then began moving off. As he was doing this he said quietly, "I'll be waitin' whenever he figures he's got to kill me, Mister Cromwell, an' meanwhile, maybe you'd tell him if he likes, I'll also start waitin' for Jute and Texas Harkins the next time they drift your cattle over on to us. Let's go, Rube; let's go Eulalia."

They walked through the crowd without any difficulty; people stepped back readily to make way, but a hundred feet farther along a burly man with a badly flattened nose and scars down around his uncompromising mouth, barred their further progress. He had a little shiny circlet on his shirt-front, with a small star inside the circlet. The way he was standing, both hands on his hips, pulled his coat aside so they could see that badge.

"Just a moment, folks," he said gruffly. "What was that all about, up there?"

"The man made a rude remark," explained Little Bob. "This here's my sister-in-law an' my brother. My name's Bob Tollman. This here is Reuben an' Eulalia, Marshal."

The scarred man ran a slow, cold look over them all as he continued to stand there, hands on hips, blocking their way. He finally glanced back up where the crowd was beginning to drift away. He said, "Boys; when you come to town let's try not to have trouble with folks. All right?"

"He didn't look for trouble," Eulalia said, standing

48

close to Reuben. "It was Mister Bowman. He deliberately bumped me, then said—that."

"All right, lady," said the marshal, looking at big Reuben. "All right. Don't fret. It's all over now. But if you folks'd leave your feuds t'home when you come to town it'd sure make things quieter around Newton." He looked Little Bob up and down one more time then brushed on past, heading up where Benton Cromwell was talking to several rangemen.

The Tollmans slowly walked back down to the livery barn. On the way Reuben said forlornly, "It wasn't a good idea after all, comin' to town."

Eulalia reached, and squeezed his hand. "It was a fine idea," she said, "wasn't it, Bob?"

The younger man looked down and nodded. "Fine," he echoed, and held out his right hand. The knuckles had been scraped raw over something and were puffy with dried blood. "The second time I missed," he explained, "and hit his belt-buckle."

They hitched up without seeing Brice Fennelly, climbed to the high seat and started northward up the back alleyway out of town. There was a black, furry sky coming down out of the north, big and swollen and low. So low in fact that it lopped the tops off all the northward lifts and rises as it advanced.

"Snow cloud," said Little Bob. "We'll have white on the ground come morning."

Reuben clucked up the team a little when they first detected that metallic scent in the air, but they made it home in plenty of time. It was while Eulalia rushed across to the house to stoke the stove that Reuben and Little Bob went into the barn with the team to unharness, and discovered that Little Bob's spotted-rump horse was missing.

They looked out back. Little Bob walked out a ways and whistled the way he sometimes did to the horse, but it wasn't in sight anywhere. He went to the house in a grim silence, brought out a lantern and held it to the ground. Reuben said, "You're not going to find anything, Bob."

His brother stopped just beyond the barn's rear opening. "No?" he said. "Come out here, Rube. There; right there. You ever seen a horse wear cowboy's boots before, Rube?"

They tracked for a ways, but when the darkness fell down from high above, dragging itself into all the nooks and crannies making even their lamp useless, there was no longer much point in going on, so they returned to the barn.

"Camp-robbers," suggested big Reuben. "Maybe some Indians passin' through."

"Sure," Little Bob murmured, gazing across the lamp at his brother. "Maybe some camp-robbers or redskins. It wasn't Cromwell or Bowman; we know that much, don't we? Let's go get some supper. Come daylight I'm goin' after him. That was the best horse I ever owned. I'm goin' after him an' I'm goin' to bring him back." Little Bob picked up the lamp and started out of the barn across towards the house. "Just the two of us are comin' back."

They went to the house and told Eulalia. She was stunned. Little Bob retired early, saying no more than he'd already said.

CHAPTER SEVEN

LITTLE BOB LEFT AHEAD OF SUNUP RIDING THE ONLY saddle horse they had left, an ageing sorrel who was slow but trustworthy.

He had his reasons for wanting to get across Cromwell range before sunup; he believed this was more harassment. He didn't believe anyone had actually stolen his horse, but had simply seen them all leave the day before and had slipped down to take away one of their prize possessions. He thought that was what had been in the minds of those two nocturnal visitors he'd spotted some time back, only that time they'd pulled out before working their mischief.

If he could be on the far side of the Cromwell outfit's range by sunup, he thought he just might be able to get someone to lead him to his horse with the spotted rump.

It was a fair guess. On the large cow outfits work was parcelled out each morning around the breakfast table, with a dark sky outside, and a glow of lamps inside. What a man lying out in the frost-stiff dead grass had to decide was which pair of riders to follow, for almost invariably when the work was handed out, it was given to the men in pairs, and they saddled up and rode off in all different directions.

He let them go south and easterly because he'd just come up from those directions and hadn't seen any livestock at all, either horses or cattle. He watched one pair of men go north and another pair head northwest. While he was debating about those two sets of riders, a solitary horseman reined out of the barn, walked his

51

horse two hundred feet to the southwest, then booted the beast over into a little lope.

There was no special reason for suspecting this one was his man, actually, but it was a feeling he had, so he went back, mounted up, turned the old sorrel and went jogging southwesterly also.

When the sun arose Little Bob was a long way back. The man he was following had an excellent mount under him. Also, the BC cowboy knew the country. He seemed to be heading into some brakes which Bob and Reuben had hunted a couple of times earlier in the fall. Bob halted to recall the lie of the onward land, then angled more southerly than westerly to enable him to reach that broken land to the south while the Cromwell man was pushing ahead from the north.

He made it, but of course the Cromwell cowboy had been down in there a half-hour ahead of him. To Little Bob that didn't mean a thing. What intrigued him was what kept the man in this place, for he'd been watching for the cowboy to come out the far side of the brakes, but the man never did.

He angled back and forth through the crooked arroyos for a while then tied the sorrel to a chaparral bush and went onward afoot, holding his scattergun across his body with both hands.

Despite the sunlight this whole area was gloomy and cold. It was as though those black clouds of the evening before had fallen into the gulches here, keeping them forever darkened. Also, there was a sound to the vagrant winds which invaded this place, like a distant moaning, which troubled a stalking man. There was of course the consoling thought that if they made Bob's nerves crawl, these sounds and dark sights, they'd also cover up any noises he might make.

Twice he climbed to low ridges to make sure the Cromwell cowboy hadn't dusted it out of this place leaving Bob still down in there. Twice he slid back down again, satisfied this hadn't happened. He didn't speculate much on what might bring a rangerider into a place such as this; he was too otherwise occupied, but when he passed around an eroded sandstone spire the color of rusty iron, he had an answer thrust upon him. There was a little band of sleek horses grazing on some grass up ahead, wearing the BC brand on the left shoulder. One horse was being kept off by the others. They didn't chase him nor make any real attempts to kick him, but whenever he'd move over to be friendly, because he was strange to the others, they'd bare their teeth and flatten their little ears at him.

It was the spotted-rump horse!

Little Bob passed back behind the rusty-red spire and took a moment to consider the condition of his horse. Evidently the animal had been led over here rather than ridden, and as far as Little Bob could determine from that distance and in that bad light, he wasn't harmed in any way.

Then the cowboy came pacing along, smoking a cigarette and with his sheepskin coat flapping loosely. He had a lariat in one hand. The horses fidgeted at that sight but made no real move to run. Cromwell's man moved into the blank place between the herd, and the Appaloosa horse. He shook out a little loop and flicked it a couple of times to get some kinks out, then he faced towards the animal with the spotted rump.

Little Bob moved from behind the dusty sandstone spire. "Steady, mister," he called, but he startled the cowboy so badly the man dropped his rope and whipped around, his right hand streaking backward and downwards.

Little Bob fired off one barrel from a distance of two hundred feet; any closer and he'd have torn the cowboy in two, and impact would have knocked him twenty feet. As it happened now, though, the widening pattern of lead pellets peppered the man nearly the full length of his body, but there was no shocking power. The cowboy still completed his draw, still fired off one round before his vision seemed to blur and his strength began to ebb away, making him stagger. He tried to raise his gun-hand for another shot, but the gun was becoming too heavy; it dragged him forward. He fell to his knees, put out one hand as the ground came up, missed and fell flat.

Little Bob remained back by his rusty spire, broke the scattergun and replaced the empty casing with a charged shell. He dropped the spent casing into a coat pocket and waited for the agitated horses to get quiet again. A shotgun made considerable noise, particularly when it was fired at close quarters in a cramped, walled-in place like this was. He didn't know that dying man over there; couldn't recall even seeing him before on the range or down in Newton, although he thought he knew all the Cromwell riders.

Eventually, with the horses milling a little but losing their wild-eyed look, Bob went on over, knelt, and leaned upon his scattergun as he one-handedly rolled the Cromwell man over.

The man wasn't dead, although by all rights he should have been. He had so many little red splotches on his body, and in some places they were so close together, it seemed incredible he'd lived this long.

"Smoke," he gasped, and Little Bob, who didn't use tobacco, rummaged the dying man's pockets, found what he was after, made a cigarette and lit it, then propped it between the man's lips.

It was cold down in this place. The cowboy's blood congealed before it dripped to the ground. His eyes assumed a very dry, still expression. Little Bob thought twice the man had died, but each time he dragged on the smoke and exhaled. He said, "Emigrant; fine-lookin' horse. I don't—blame you."

Bob inclined his head. "Good horse, sure. But no horse's worth gettin' killed over, mister. Why'd you draw?"

The man's dry gaze was turning cloudy when he said, "A feller don't want to be hung for a—horsethief, emigrant. Anyway—who ever heard of a clod-hopper—beatin' a tophand to the—draw?"

"Was it Ned's idea, runnin' off my horse, mister?"

The cowboy enigmatically smiled with his lips and died without answering. Little Bob hunkered there for a while gazing at the man; he'd been young, about Bob's own age, and he'd been pleasant looking, friendly, willing. It was a waste, Little Bob thought; a waste of a man's life for that rangerider to cash in like this.

He went back-tracking the man until he found his horse, then he took it back, tied the cowboy across it, tied his sixgun with its one empty casing securely to the saddlehorn, checked the horse up so it couldn't get its head down to graze, and gave it a light pat on the rump.

He switched his outfit from the sorrel to the spotted-rump horse and rode up out of the brakes heading straight eastward. He was just about parallel with the claim, he thought.

For a while he had the BC horse with its grisly burden in sight, but when the day began to fog up with low clouds again as had happened the day before in the afternoon, he lost sight of the beast.

It was dusk before he got back to the claim, although

55

it actually was still mid-afternoon. He put up both horses and went back to lean in the rear doorway for a while, gazing northwesterly. By now Cromwell, Bowman, everyone on the BC ranch, had seen that dead man. He speculated on their reactions, over there, and thought it very likely they'd come riding this night. Cromwell he wasn't certain of, but he knew Ned Bowman; if it were left to the rangeboss, he'd come with the entire BC crew and loaded for bear.

Across the darkening yard there was the warm and inviting glow of lamplight. Reuben and Eulalia would be sitting down to supper. They wouldn't know when to expect him back any more than they'd have any idea where he went or what he'd done. That had its advantages and although he'd miss another meal, he had some jerky in a pocket he hadn't touched all day long, so he'd manage quite well, as he watched and waited.

But it didn't work out like that, for Reuben came down to feed and restlessly stamp about, and saw the spotted-rump horse and the old sorrel. He then climbed to the loft and saw Little Bob lying up there with the loft doors cracked a little, his scattergun shoved out.

He came over and hunkered down looking out through the cold darkness. "You couldn't see anyone out there," he quietly said, "if they were carrying torches. What happened, Bob?"

"I got my horse back, Rube."

"I saw him down there."

"And I killed one of Cromwell's riders."

" . . .Oh."

"Fair enough fight, Reuben. He went for his belt-gun and I cut him down at a couple of hundred feet; maybe a little more."

"You left him lying?"

"No; that's why I'm waitin' up here now. I tied him across his horse and sent him on home. By now they have him. They've had enough time to about get over here too. Rube; you go on back to the house an' stay with Eulalia. They may not even come. I don't know how some folks react to a killin'. All the same, go on back and don't say anything about me being back yet. No sense in gettin' Eulalia all upset."

Reuben stood up, he reached, pushed one loft door a little and peered out into the lowering night. The same metallic scent was there again. "Snow by mornin'," he murmured absently, and went over to the ladder down out of the loft. "You got food up here, Bob?"

"Yeah. Turn out that lamp in there, Rube, or hang a blanket over the window."

Reuben finished climbing down. Little Bob heard him halt in the middle of their big barn, then start moving again, shuffling towards the yonder yard and the cabin on across there a ways.

He was warm enough in the loft hay. He wasn't freezing at least, and the hay was both fragrant and soft to lie upon. Then too, it was so dark up there even when he held up his own hand, he couldn't see it, so he was safe enough from anyone slipping into the barn and coming up behind him.

Once, he heard horses out there on the westerly plain, but they seemed to be rushing southward, not eastward towards the claim. Another time he heard two owls hooting back and forth from a distance of not more than a hundred yards. But evidently they were real owls, not men, because that's all there was to it; a little hooting, then silence.

He began to think perhaps he'd misjudged Bowman and Cromwell, or that perhaps they weren't going to hit the claim until daylight. When his toes began to tingle along towards dawn he got up and stamped up and down the loft, leaving his scattergun where it lay in the loft opening over there.

He speculated on why nothing had happened. Of all the notions he had the least plausible one was that the horse bearing the dead cowboy had ambled around in the dark and hadn't gotten to the ranch until it was too late for the men to be abroad. He knew better than to believe that; he'd seen the horse heading straight home himself, and with ample daylight left, too.

There came a streak of icy blue light across the top of the world enabling him to see a mile outward; where there should have been BC riders, armed and grim-faced, there was nothing but a world layered over with black frost. He went over, scooped up his shotgun, stiffly descended from the loft and stood a moment swinging his arms vigorously, and turned and went stamping across the frozen yard towards the house where a thin spiral of dark smoke was rising straight up into the steely dawn.

CHAPTER EIGHT

LITTLE BOB GOT HIS ANSWER BY TEN O'CLOCK, WITH that leaden sky lingering this time, not departing as it had the day before, and with the world as far as any of them could see, curled in death from the first black frost of the autumn.

The deputy U.S. marshal rode into the yard accompanied by Benton Cromwell. Reuben saw them coming long before they reached the yard. He told Eulalia, it might not be a bad idea to set some coffee to boil, then he walked outside with Little Bob to catch the riders over at the barn where the tie-rack stood. Reuben wasn't armed. Little Bob was, both with a belt-gun under his coat, and the shotgun draped over his right arm.

The lawman recognized the Tollmans at once, evidently, because he gently nodded his head as they came across to where he and Cromwell stood. "Good mornin', fellers," he said affably, and began unbuttoning his coat although it was very cold out. "I got warrants for your arrest."

Little Bob stopped, put his clear stare upon Cromwell and said, "Who signed the warrants, Marshal; Mister Cromwell?"

"As a matter of fact he did, boys."

"How?" asked Little Bob. "He didn't see it happen."

"Well now, Mister Tollman," said the deputy U.S. marshal, his scarred brows puckering a little with mild annoyance. "I never seen a battleship in my life because I've never seen an ocean, but I'm right sure there are both big oceans an' battleships in this world."

Reuben's brow puckered. "Warrants?" he asked the lawman. "Does that mean the both of us, Marshal?"

"It sure does, Mister Tollman. The both of you are under arrest for murder."

Reuben's troubled eyes widened. "Murder, Marshal . . . ?"

"Yes sir, Mister Tollman: Murder. I've seen the body; it was riddled with buckshot. I've seen the man's gun; it was clean as a whistle and hadn't been fired in a week or longer."

Little Bob stood perfectly still gazing at Benton Cromwell. The big cowman looked straight back. Little Bob said softly, "Marshal; you should've ridden on over where it happened. You'd have picked up just one set of tracks—mine. My brother never left the claim. His wife'll tell you that."

The deputy marshal, whose name was Howard Mather, gave his shoulders a little loose shrug. "Tollman," he said to Little Bob, "I still got two warrants."

"In that case," drawled Little Bob, "I withdraw everything I just said."

"You—what?"

"You heard me, Marshal; I withdraw everything I just told you. Now let you'n Benton Cromwell prove I was over there and killed that man of his. I'll deny it right down the line, and without a single witness, you're goin' to have to do a heap of convincin', Marshal, to make it stick."

The lawman gazed up at Benton Cromwell, who was a taller man. He had a rueful look on his face as he waited for Cromwell to speak up. It wasn't much of a wait. Cromwell said, "All right, Deputy, forget the older one. Take that one with the shotgun."

Mather held out a hand. Little Bob didn't hesitate; he handed across his shotgun, reached under his coat and pulled out the belt-gun, then he said, "Mister Cromwell; one time back home I heard a lawyer say a man'd who help conceal a crime is equally as guilty as the man who committed it. Why did you tell the marshal this was murder?"

"It *was* murder!"

"You're a liar, Mister Cromwell. Why didn't you leave that pistol the way you found it tied to the saddlehorn? I'll answer for you: because this way you can make your play at forcing us off the land . . . Marshal; that cowboy fired at me. I tied his pistol to the

60

saddlehorn so's Cromwell and Bowman would see that's how it was."

"Sure," said the lawman, turning to tie Bob's shotgun to his saddle. "Mister Tollman; I don't hold no court. I only make the arrests and fetch 'em in for trial. If what you say's the truth, then the court'll more than likely find it out."

Eulalia came out and called across that she had hot coffee. Marshal Mather looked at the rancher and Cromwell shook his head, turned his back to Eulalia and got astride his horse.

The lawman removed his hat, gallantly thanked Eulalia but said they'd like to return to Newton ahead of the storm. She went back inside.

Big Reuben went into the barn to saddle Bob's spotted-rump horse, and Little Bob stayed out there in front of the lawman and Benton Cromwell, as silent and impassive as an Indian.

The deputy marshal regarded Little Bob for a long moment before he said, "Why, Tollman; what was the reason you done it?"

"He had my horse, Marshal."

"You mean he stole him?"

"I don't know who stole him. I didn't see that happen. All I know is that when we got back to the claim yesterday after being in town, my horse was gone."

"He could've strayed, Tollman."

Little Bob gazed at the law officer. "With his halter-shank tied to the hole in the manger?"

Cromwell said, "Tollman; it doesn't matter how your horse got on to my range. He was there. One of my boys found him there—but you were with him. Now, my man is dead and no one is around to tell us exactly what happened but you."

"And you," stated Little Bob. "Just tell the truth about the gun, Mister Cromwell. It had one bullet fired from it—at me. I tied it to the saddlehorn exactly as I picked it up after your cowboy went down. Then I sent him back to you."

"That was kind of dumb," muttered the lawman, craning around to see what was taking Reuben so long inside the barn.

Little Bob gazed at the lawman. "I didn't want to hide anything," he said. "Maybe you think I was dumb not to, but I don't fight by stealth, Marshal. I wanted Cromwell to know I'd found out about him having my horse stolen exactly as I'd found out about him having his BC cattle drifted over on to our grass, deliberately."

Cromwell didn't comment; he simply sat up there looking caustic and gently shaking his head. Reuben came forth leading the spotted-rump horse. He handed the reins to his brother. "I'll be in directly," he said. "You take care, hear?"

Little Bob turned, stepped across leather and let Benton Cromwell ride off ahead of him. Howard Mather came up beside Bob and said, "What about the cattle you were mentioning?" Little Bob explained as they rode out of the yard easterly towards the stageroad, and was just finishing his recitation when Benton Cromwell, several hundred feet ahead, turned and held out one hand. It was beginning to snow.

The lawman turned up his coat collar, buttoned up to the throat and pulled his hat down low in front of his face. He rode along eyeing Benton Cromwell's broad back, saying nothing more until, with the flakes lazily drifting down faster and larger at the outskirts of town, Cromwell would have reined off towards a saloon which lay on the upper east side of the main

62

thoroughfare, then Mather called after him, telling Cromwell he wanted him to ride on down to the jailhouse with the pair of them.

"The warrant is signed," said Cromwell, turning irritable. "You don't need me any more, Deputy."

"Oh but I do need more," said Mather, sounding a lot milder than he looked. "You told me what you figured happened an' on the strength o' that I made the arrest, but now what I need is your signed deposition. Otherwise, Mister Cromwell, I can't hold this man fifteen minutes." Mather smiled broadly. "Sometimes fellers are downright mean about bein' hauled in an' held a spell, then turned loose."

Cromwell turned his horse and went on down the roadway on Mather's far side, dour and resentful. There were few people out now because the snow was coming thicker and heavier. Somewhere over on a back road several boys were loudly whooping over the first snowfall of the winter, but except for that there didn't appear to be any other elation; certainly the merchants weren't delighted, nor the housewives who'd now have six months of cleaning up puddles and trying to dry carpets in an atmosphere which wouldn't be dry again until the following summer.

At the liverybarn Marshal Mather stiffly climbed down and handed his reins to a hostler. He idly asked where Brice Fennelly was, learned the liveryman was over at the café with a couple of friends, and told the hostler to also take charge of Bob Tollman's horse. He then led the grim-faced men on each side of him up through the soft-falling snow to the jailhouse, and there, as he poked some life into a little iron stove, Benton Cromwell sat at the desk writing out his charges against Bob Tollman. He was signing it when Little Bob said,

"Mister Cromwell; it's sort of disappointin'. The cattle bein' slyly drifted over to eat our feed I understood. The cold-shoulder in town from BC cowboys we expected, 'cause after all, we're only emigrants. Maybe even havin' that feller steal my horse to harass us some more, was more of the same." Little Bob pointed at the paper Cromwell was poised to sign. "But that two-page lie you're tellin' there about me murdering your cowboy— that's a lot different. You're fixin' to try'n get me hung now, Mister Cromwell. That's worse than just sneakin' and lyin' and being underhanded."

"That's enough," called over the deputy marshal from where he was coaxing life into some sullen coals. "Tollman; leave off it."

Little Bob crossed to a chair, swung the thing and dropped astraddle of it, his chin resting upon both arms over the back of the chair, steadily staring at Benton Cromwell as the cowman went ahead and signed his deposition, then stood up looking over at the stove. "Anything else, Marshal?"

Mather was straightening up, frowning into his stove, as he indifferently answered. "Just one more thing, Mister Cromwell: At the ranch this morning you give me the dead man's gun. Who cleaned it?"

Cromwell snapped up straight. "You're saying you believe this man when he says he was fired at, Marshal."

Mather was shorter than both the big men in his office, but as he now turned to gaze over at them both, there wasn't the least bit of fear in his scarred face. Even though he certainly knew who Benton Cromwell was, he eyed the wealthy cowman with the same brimstone look also turned upon his prisoner.

"Mister Cromwell," he said evenly, "all I did was ask

64

you a simple question. All I want is a simple answer. Then, you see, someone's got to be lyin', and I'll find out who he is. Now tell me—who cleaned that gun before I got there this morning?"

"No one cleaned it!" stormed Cromwell, and stamped to the door, yanked it open, went out, and slammed it after himself.

Little Bob sat where he was, watching the deputy marshal coaxing life into his little iron stove. Once, Mather turned, met the younger man's look, and returned to his work making some complainingly garrulous comments about his stove. For Little Bob the deputy marshal was a genuine enigma. He never seemed to be thinking the way he looked, nor seemed ready to react the way he predictably should have reacted. Little Bob had never before encountered a man quite like Howard Mather; as clever as Bob was at seeing through what was on the outside of men, this time he was having difficulty. Mather was scarred and pounded from many battles. He was an almost affable man at his work, and he never seemed to be thinking of crimes; then he'd up and ask some question like the one he'd just asked Benton Cromwell; a two-edged question which made a liar out of a man no matter which way he answered it.

Mather finally got the fire crackling, closed the door, set the flue with a delicate touch, then stood back like a craftsman admiring his work. "It's as tempermental as a woman," he said, turning to cross to the desk, squint at Cromwell's hand-written deposition, then begin shedding his sheepskin coat. "But it'll warm the place up right now, Mister Tollman." He hung up the coat, sat down, swung around and gestured. "Shed your coat, Mister Tollman; directly, when she gets to poppin', I'll set the coffee pot on an' we'll have a nice little visit."

He paused, reared back, peered out a little grilled window, then rocked forward again shaking his head. "That damned stuff'll be a foot deep directly. Good thing I got a couple tier of wood out back." He fished out a tobacco sack and packet of rice-straw papers. "Smoke?" he said. Bob shook his head. "Bad habit all right," conceded Howard Mather, then went right to work with both hands to prove that he possessed such a bad habit.

"You ever see that man you killed before?" he shot at Little Bob, lighting up, then snapping the match.

"No. I'm right sure of that, too."

"Good. How'd you know where to find him?"

"Shagged him. Lay atop a little swell northwest o' the Cromwell place come sunup, watched 'em all ride out. He was the only loner, an' he went about in the right direction, so I shagged him. He rode into some broken land, I hid my horse, took the scattergun, and went a-huntin' him. When we met he was fixin' to rope my horse. I called him an' the damned fool, instead of standin' steady, he went for his gun. I shot him, but he was pretty fast. He still got off one shot at me, an' tried to get off another one before he went down."

"Was he dead?"

"No. I made him a smoke. He smiled."

"What did he say?"

"Nothing much. I asked who sent him to get my horse; he died about then."

The marshal sat there smoking for a while, then he got up, jerked his head towards a pair of identical strapsteel cages along the back of the room, and hiked over to unlock one of them. "Be pleasant enough for tonight," he said, as Little Bob walked in. "Snowin' up a blizzard outside, a fire inside, I'll fetch you some

66

coffee directly, later on supper, then sleep, with the stove cracklin' and poppin'." He smiled in but Little Bob didn't smile out.

It was turning dark now, although it was scarcely past midday. Dark and hushed and with a brimstone tang to the storm-roiled air.

CHAPTER NINE

BRICE FENNELLY CAME OVER AND SAT WITH THE deputy U.S. marshal for a while, sipping coffee and smoking. Now and then those two would try to draw Little Bob out of his solemn silence, but failed. Then Brice left and the deputy marshal went out to fetch a tray of supper for his prisoner.

There was a skiff of snow everywhere. It muffled all sound, even when riders came jogging in from the ranches for some nightly entertainment.

Later, after Bob had eaten, he had two visitors. The first one was big Reuben, but Rube didn't linger long because, as he said, he didn't like leaving Eulalia out there all by herself, and unless he struck out for home directly, if the consarned storm kept up, he'd likely have a tarnation time making it. He left a battered old family Bible with Little Bob.

As soon as Rube left, Little Bob handed the Bible out to Marshal Mather. "Set it aside," he said. "I'll take it back with me when I go home."

"Sure," Mather assented, and placed the dog-eared old book atop his desk. "Aren't you a believin' man, Tollman?" he asked.

Bob nodded. "Yeah, Marshal, I'm a believin' man. I'm just not a *beggin'* one."

67

The second visitor was Benton Cromwell himself, which was a surprise to both the marshal and his prisoner. Cromwell was gruff and brusque. He wanted to talk to the prisoner alone. Howard Mather was agreeable to that, and shrugged into his coat then went outside.

Cromwell was a large, handsome, well-fed-looking man, who always gave the impression he was capable of handling anything which came up. He stood outside Little Bob's cell gazing in now, and Bob detected the troubled shadows in the background of Cromwell's blue stare.

"Tollman," the cowman said, "I can get you out of here. Get the whole thing tossed out. I'm willing to do that in exchange for your word you'll take that damned Appaloosa horse and go away; get out of the country and don't come back."

Little Bob sat down on the pallet inside his cell, set his hat aside, stretched out his long legs, folded both arms under his head, and stared unwaveringly without saying a word.

For a while Cromwell weathered it, then he said, "Listen, Tollman; I'm giving you a chance for your life. If you want to lie back there playing games it's all right with me. But by next week at this time you'll very likely be standin' on a scaffold for murder."

"I didn't murder anyone," Little Bob retorted, "and you know it, Mister Cromwell."

"Then listen to me, Tollman; pass me your word you'll—"

"I wouldn't pass you my word on anything, Mister Cromwell," said Little Bob. "But I'll make you a promise; if you don't get me hanged, I'll kill both you and Bowman as soon as I'm out of here."

Little Bob reached, dropped his hat down over his face and seemed to wish to sleep. Benton Cromwell stood a moment looking into the cell, then turned with an oath and slammed out of the jailhouse.

As soon as the deputy marshal returned, he went over to the cell, unbuttoned his sheepskin coat and said, "Hey; don't play 'possum with me, boy, you're no more asleep than she was."

Little Bob reached out, lifted the hat and said, "She, Marshal?"

"Yeah. Sarah Cromwell."

Little Bob put the hat aside, swung his legs to the floor and stood up. "I never knew that," he told the lawman. "I always heard he was a bachelor."

"He is a bachelor. She's his niece. Come to live with him last year about the time I hit this country. His only livin' kin so the story goes. There's another story too; when she wants something he gets it for her. Now then, Mister Tollman; when I stepped outside to leave you'n Cromwell together— there she was, pretty as the picture on a calendar, standin' out yonder in the snow, waitin' for her uncle to come out and tell her it was all arranged."

Little Bob said, "Arranged . . . ?"

"Sure, boy; don't tell me Cromwell didn't offer to get you off the hook if you'd go away an' stay away?"

Little Bob nodded.

"That's it exactly."

The marshal looked wry, "What'd you expect? He wants you so far off Sarah won't even remember what you look like."

Bob went back and sat down. He'd had it figured entirely another way; he was certain Cromwell wanted him out of the way so he could step up the harassment against Reuben and Eulalia. Marshal Mather stood out

69

there, thumbs hooked in his belt, gazing thoughtfully in at Little Bob. After a while he gave his shoulders a shake and went to his desk, sat down, took a sixgun out of a desk drawer and sat for a full ten minutes just looking at it.

When it was close to midnight Little Bob, who'd had no sleep the night before and very little the night before that, asked when Mather was going home; when he would turn out the cussed light on his desk which shone straight into Little Bob's eyes. Mather only grunted something about Little Bob covering his eyes with his hat, and went on examining that gun in his hands.

It was nearly midnight before the lawman got up, yawned mightily, then went over to make a fresh pot of coffee. Little Bob fell asleep feeling resentful and smoldering, feeling nearly as resentful towards Howard Mather as against Benton Cromwell.

At one o'clock someone came stamping into the office making enough noise to wake the dead. Little Bob sat up balefully looking out through his bars. The newcomer, bundled to the ears and wearing bearskin gauntlets wasn't recognizable until he shed his coat, two sweaters beneath the coat, a big furry muffler and his bearskin gloves. It was Brice Fennelly and he had a lariat neatly coiled in his hands which he wordlessly handed to the marshal, then stamped more snow off his boots and hiked over to get himself a tin cup full of black coffee.

Mather put aside the sixgun which had been occupying his attention, parted the lariat at the loop, looked around where Brice was standing, chilled to the bone, and raised his eyebrows. Fennelly grunted, walked over and fished something out of a shirt pocket

70

which Little Bob couldn't make out, and handed it to the lawman also.

Finally, Marshal Mather smiled. "Quite a night for ridin' out," he said to the liveryman, and that calm comment elicited a sizzling oath from Fennelly who stalked back over by the stove to bend a little, warming his backside.

Little Bob stood up, grabbed his bars and said in a sleep-hoarsened voice, "Mister Mather; if you're goin' to keep me awake all night, how about another cup of that java?"

He didn't get it. Howard Mather strolled over to the cell, still smiling, and said, "That man you shot, Mister Tollman; did you notice something odd about him?"

Little Bob said, "Yeah; somethin' real odd. He was tryin' to kill me."

Mather's sunk-set eyes cooled a little from their former sly warmth. "Very funny," he mumbled. "Let's try it again—he was left-handed, Tollman. Did you notice that?"

"Yes. That's not very odd. You can see left-handed folks every day if you watch for them."

Mather held up the coiled lariat. "This is the rope you tied him on his horse with."

Little Bob shrugged; one hard-twist lariat looked like any other, coiled or uncoiled. Mather pushed it through the bars. "Uncoil it," he said. "Go ahead; don't stand there lookin' stupid. Uncoil it." Little Bob obeyed. The rope had been coiled back left-handed again. He tested its turns to be certain of this, then handed it back through the bars.

"What of it?" he asked.

"Benton Cromwell is also left-handed. Did you happen to notice that?" Bob replied candidly that he

71

hadn't noticed that; that he'd only seen Cromwell three or four times and the cowman had always had a coat on so Bob couldn't be sure which side Cromwell wore his gun on. "But what of it?" he demanded. "I just said, lots of men are—"

"Cromwell and Bowman told me it was Bowman who found the dead man and took him off the horse you'd tied him on. Bowman's right-handed. If he'd re-coiled this rope, Tollman, it'd have been coiled reverse to what it is."

Bob began to lower his brows in a puzzled way. From over at the stove Brice Fennelly said, "Cromwell was lyin', Bob. Bowman didn't find the dead man— Cromwell did."

Mather nodded. "Exactly. Now then; the question is: Why did Cromwell lie? Another question is: If he lied to me once, what would keep him from lyin' to me right down the line?"

Little Bob was mystified. He couldn't imagine what difference it made who'd stolen his horse, or why Cromwell had lied about finding the dead cowboy. But he said, "Marshal; I told him he was lyin' to his face when you were standin' right there, which I know for a fact is gospel truth."

Mather pulled a little flattened lead slug out of his pocket and held it on his palm. "Brice rode out in the blizzard and got this slug out of the spire you were standin' beside when you and that dead cowboy swapped lead, Tollman."

Little Bob's eyes widened at Fennelly. The liveryman's bluish color was slowly changing back to its normal ruddy red. He said, "I didn't volunteer, Li'l Bob. The marshal made me do it."

"But why?" Bob wanted to know, bringing his glance back to Mather.

The lawman blandly smiled. "Well: y'see, that dog-goned Brice once before tried to get some folks to keep Cromwell's cattle off his land out there by leasin' the land so's others would do his arguin' for him. That time, the emigrants just chucked the whole thing and left the country. This time, a man died. When he came in a while back—after I sent word down to the barn I wanted to see him—we made a little trade; he'd do some ridin' out in the blizzard for me, and in return I'd not jail him for incitin' trouble."

Little Bob began to get the drift of all this. He gazed from Brice Fennelly to the lawman, his expression showing a slow-dawning comprehension. He said, in his quiet Kentucky drawl, "Marshal; I never made such a bad guess about a man before in my life. You sure just never hit me as that sly a feller."

Mather chuckled. "Never judge a book by its cover," he said, and turned. "Brice; you did a good lick tonight. How's the weather out?"

Fennelly's answer to that was fiercely profane as he turned to pour himself another cup of hot black coffee.

Mather considered the slug in his palm, pocketed it and strolled back to his desk, picked up the sixgun lying there and hefted the thing for a moment before returning it to a desk drawer. Then he said, "Now listen to me, the both of you; don't breathe a word of this to anyone. Tollman; if that big ox of a brother shows up tomorrow—not a word even to him. And Brice, if you—"

"You think," exploded the liveryman, "I did all that skulkin' around in the snow half froze to death, just to see it all undone?" Fennelly filled a second cup with coffee, crossed the room and offered the cup through the bars to Little Bob. "All right," he said, in a lower tone.

73

"You pegged me right about the land out there, Li'l Bob. I wasn't doin' anyone any favours by leasin' it to you folks for practically nothin', but myself. An' you were right about what you said the other day at the barn —I didn't want to tangle with Benton Cromwell if I could get someone else to do it for me. Here; take the coffee, this damned tin cup's gettin' hot. All right; I'll make it up. You just name the price."

Marshal Mather waited, but when Little Bob sipped coffee and balefully, wordlessly regarded the liveryman, Mather said, "He's not as much to blame as you think, Tollman. Tomorrow, with any luck, maybe we can get the right men settled up with. After all, what Brice did was more sly than hurtful but what Bowman and Cromwell tried to do to you—well—that's what I'd like to see straightened out."

Bob looked across Fennelly's shoulder. "How?" he demanded.

But Mather didn't answer. He just put the left-handed lariat on his desk and said, "Brice; go on home. It's late an' tomorrow maybe we'll be busy, if Cromwell comes to town like I'm sure he will."

The liveryman turned so fast he nearly spilled the remainder of his coffee. "We," he exclaimed. "Where do you get that 'we' business, Howard? I agreed to go hunt up the bullet and steal the lariat for you—in this lousy blizzard—but that's my end of it."

Mather yawned and went over to his office lamp as though to blow down the mantle. "Not quite," he told the liveryman, looking Brice Fennelly straight in the eye, no longer smiling. "You're involved in the killing of that BC cowboy, Brice, whether you think so or not. You can make your mind up to a couple of things right here an' now: Either you help undo what you've done to the Tollmans, not to mention those other folks last year, or I'm goin' to prefer charges myself an' put you in the same cell with Mister Tollman."

Fennelly stood with his jaw sagging. "I thought we were friends," he said reproachfully.

Mather's lips quirked in a hard, mirthless smile. "Oh we *are*," he said. "That's why I'm doin' it this way. The other way—prison maybe, for incitin' a killing, deceivin' settlers, circumventin' the law."

Fennelly swore again and looked helplessly around at Little Bob. He got nothing there but a cold stare. He went over to the stove, put his empty cup down, hard, and scooped his coat and muffler. From over by the door he glared and said, "Damn you, Howard; you're deliberately forcin' me into facin' Benton Cromwell, an' you know it as well as I do."

Mather shrugged, still poised to blow out the lamp. "It's good for the backbone," he murmured. "Anyway; you'd have to face him sooner or later, over that piece of land. Tomorrow'll be just the day for it. Go on out now, I'm goin' to put out the light." Fennelly departed, Marshal Mather solemnly winked over at Little Bob, then blew, and the jailhouse was plunged into an eerie, snow-glaring darkness.

CHAPTER TEN

CROMWELL DIDN'T SHOW UP IN NEWTON THE NEXT morning. In fact no one from the outlying ranches rode in, the snow was almost fourteen inches deep and unless it was a matter of life and death, no one would make the effort.

Deputy U.S. Marshal Howard Mather played pinochle

through the bars with his prisoner, and when Brice Fennelly came in the lawman sent him over to the café for a tray for his prisoner. Fennelly went, but he made a face about it, and when he returned he said Howard was purposefully picking on him.

The marshal cheerfully admitted that this was the truth, then they all sat down and played three-handed poker, while outside whooping boys thoroughly enjoyed the blizzard, but they—and the deputy U.S. marshal—seemed to be the only people who did enjoy it.

When the snow ceased it was nearly midday. That event brought a few venturesome souls out to scowl at the sky, but the roadway was still empty. Not until the northbound stage came slogging through four hours late, did the roadway lose its virginal smoothness. After that, along towards early evening, four riders appeared coming out of the grey-misty north country, their horses staying in the ruts the coach had made. Those four had a little conversation over in front of a saloon, then parted, two of them stiffly getting down to tie up out front of the barroom, the other pair sloshing on down towards the jailhouse.

Marshal Mather, Brice Fennelly and the prisoner were still at their three-handed poker when the roadway door opened, Benton Cromwell stamped in, and right behind him came Ned Bowman, his ivory-butted sixgun visible as soon as Ned, responding to the heat of the room, unbuttoned his sheepskin rider's coat.

Howard Mather glanced unhappily at his hand of cards, tossed them down and got up to go over near the door where his visitors remained, balefully eyeing the prisoner, who only very briefly glanced up, once, in their direction, then lowered his head and resumed his card game. Brice Fennelly did the same, but right

76

afterwards Brice lost a pot containing eleven cents simply because, despite his impassivity, he got rattled and pitched away the wrong card when he called for a replacement.

"Hard day for ridin' in," said the lawman to Benton Cromwell. "Unless of course a man's got a real good reason."

Cromwell ignored the marshal, crossed over and stared in at Little Bob. "Did you think over what I told you yesterday?" he asked.

Little Bob gazed at Brice Fennelly, saying, "Blackjack's better for just two players; want to switch over, same stakes?"

Fennelly painfully swallowed, and nodded. He reached to rack up the cards and shuffle. Ned Bowman stepped in close and put forth a gloved hand as though to stop the dealing. Howard Mather, still between the door and his desk, with his hands hanging straight down, said, "Ned; leave 'em be."

Bowman's hand stopped moving. He turned his swarthy face. Mather was standing relaxed and slouched. They exchanged a long look, then the lawman straightened up slowly, and just as slowly walked across to halt five feet off. "Back up," he said very mildly to Cromwell's rangeboss. "Around here you do what *I* say; on Cromwell range you don't—but in here you'd better believe it when I say you'll do as I say. Now back off!" The last three words were ripped out.

Benton Cromwell raised a hand at his foreman, looking annoyed. "Leave them be," he said. "I'll handle this, Ned."

Finally, the swarthy rangeboss moved back, and as he did so, Brice Fennelly's Adam's apple gave a leap and a dip. Little Bob hadn't looked up throughout all that dangerous moment, but now he did. He gazed out at Brice and said, "Deal!"

Cromwell stepped closer and leaned upon the back of the chair Howard Mather had been using. "Just a minute," he said to Fennelly. "This won't take long, but I've got to get it out into words. Tollman; if you'll do what I said last night when we talked alone, I'll do what I said, and give you five hundred dollars to boot."

Little Bob looked straight at the liveryman. "Deal," he softly said. "Let's get on with it, Fennelly." But the liveryman, with Ned Bowman somewhere behind him and Benton Cromwell at his side, threw down the cards and shook his head. "Later maybe," he muttered, and arose to turn and move away.

Little Bob reached through to pick up the cards. "Solitaire, then," he muttered, but Benton Cromwell's hand moved swiftly to cover half the pasteboards.

"A thousand, then," the cowman said, leaning towards Little Bob.

Finally, with so few alternatives left, Little Bob lifted his head. "You don't want me out of here," he said quietly. "Because I told you yesterday, Mister Cromwell, when I get out I'm going after both you and Bowman."

Ned's head jerked forward. "Shotgun-man; I'd like that. I'd almost be willin' to go your bail just so's we could have this little meetin'."

Cromwell's temple swelled and his eyes began to smolder. He kept gazing in at Little Bob. Finally, he straightened up off the chair-back. "Tollman," he said in a silky tone. "You've had your fun just now, ignorin' me. But that's over now. You better think this over because I'm dead serious: One thousand and you ride away—and stay away."

78

Little Bob unwound up off his chair and leaned a little, both hands upon the bars while he put a blank look outward. "Get out of here, Cromwell, and take that half-breed with you. You called it last summer— enemies. You been callin' it the same way ever since. Now, all of a sudden, you got terms to offer. Well, Mister Cromwell, maybe you're through fightin', but we Tollmans haven't even begun to fight yet. Marshal; how about runnin' these two out so I can get some decent air to breathe?"

Ned Bowman's face was grey, his black eyes were like wet obsidian. When Benton Cromwell mumbled for Ned to come along, Bowman didn't hear him. Cromwell was half through the roadway door-opening before Marshal Mather strode over and deliberately bumped the rangeboss, then jerked his head.

"Your boss is waitin' for you, Bowman."

Over by the gunrack Brice Fennelly was like a permanent fixture, his eyes perfectly round as he watched Ned Bowman finally leave. Over in his cell Little Bob Tollman said, "Marshal; I thought you were goin' to nail 'em when they rode in today?"

"That's right," Mather conceded. "But when I got to listenin' to Cromwell, I got another notion."

"Yeah?" called Little Bob dryly. "Well, you better be careful; these ideas you keep getting could up an' get someone hurt."

Howard Mather looked over at the liveryman. "Brice; I thought for a while there you were goin' to faint."

Fennelly sighed and felt for a round-backed chair. "I was plumb willin', but the lousy wall held me up. Howard; did you see how Bowman looked at Li'l Bob? Like he wanted to gouge out his eyes with—"

"Why do you call a man as big as Robert Tollman,

Little Bob?" Mather went to a little window and gazed out into the ghostly roadway. Without turning, he said, "Well; why do you, Brice?"

Fennelly remembered the coffee pot and headed straight for it. "Old Southern custom," he said. "The youngest son we call either Bubba, meanin' little brother, or we just stick the 'little' in front of his reg'lar name. Now Howard; this isn't no time for a lot of tomfoolishness—"

"You're plumb right," said the marshal. "Go saddle up three stout horses, Brice, an' fetch 'em back up to the tie-rack outside." Mather turned from the window where he'd been studying the roadway. "Well," he exclaimed, staring. "What you waitin' for, an engraved invitation, Brice? Go get us them three horses."

Fennelly kept a baleful look upon the federal peace officer. "You're up to somethin'," he said in a sing-song way. "Howard; you sneaky devil, you're up to—"

"Just get the damned horses, Brice. And hurry about it, too."

"Howard; if you're includin' me again I flatly refuse to let you—"

Mather wrenched the door open. "Out, doggone it!" he snarled. "Brice, you go fetch back them three horses; an' you can bet your bottom dollar you're goin' with us. If you figure for a minute we're square just because what you did last night, you got another think comin'. Now *move*!"

Brice moved; he went out into the white cold and turned to voice one final big protest. Marshal Mather slammed the door.

Through all this Little Bob had watched, holding to the bars. Now, as the peace officer slammed the roadside door and, muttering a strong oath, walked over to his desk after a ring of keys, Bob said, "Marshal; you better be right sure you know what you're doin'.""

Mather raised his scarred face. "That's a silly thing to say," he growled. "Did you ever know a gambler who was right sure about the outcome when he started a game?" Mather ambled on over to Bob's cell with his key-ring. "You listen to me," he said, inserting the key and giving it a hard twist, unlocking the cell door. "When Cromwell and Bowman walked in here, I got an idea just from watchin' them. Now I'm going to gamble on it, and you'n Brice Fennelly are comin' with me."

Little Bob pushed open his cell door and walked out into the center of the office where he turned and put a skeptical look back over at Howard Mather. "What's this notion got to do with me?" he asked.

"Plenty," Mather cryptically answered, crossing back to his desk where he tossed down the key-ring. He was standing between Little Bob and the door. He gently shook his head. "Forget any ideas you get," he told the taller and younger man. "And I mean *any*, ideas, Bob, because even if I didn't have this gun on, you couldn't get the job done."

Little Bob gazed wonderingly at Mather. "You plumb sure of that?" he asked quietly.

"Plumb certain," exclaimed the deputy U.S. marshal. "But for right now let's do this differently: Tollman; I want your word you'll stay with me tonight and do exactly as I say—no matter what you see, or what we run into. Otherwise . . ." Mather pointed back towards the cell.

Little Bob stood there eyeing the burly, shorter man. "I'm right careful about giving my word," he eventually stated. "You give me some idea what we'll be up to, and I'll turn it over in m'mind first, Marshal."

81

"We're going out to your brother's claim. 'That satisfy you, Bob?"

For a second Little Bob didn't answer, then, when he finally did respond, he was just as impassive as before, but his voice had altered a little; there was a soft-steel hardness to it. "That satisfies me, Marshal. You figure, with only my brother an' his wife out there, now, Cromwell and Bowman will make some trouble."

"Well; I'm *hoping* they will, Bob, because after I got to lookin' at those two when they first walked in a while back, I could see there wasn't a ghost of a chance o' me sweating anything out of them they didn't want to tell me. So; I hung back and listened—as you may've noticed—waitin' for something to crystallize I could use. It crystallized all right; when you called Bowman a 'breed he was teeterin' on the naked edge of shooting you down right there in your cell. And Cromwell took your refusal to consider his offer just about as hard." Mather opened the door, peeked out, closed the door and called Brice Fennelly a harsh name. Then, in his former tone of voice he said, "Those two want *you*, Tollman. They don't want your brother nor his lady. Right now they aren't even thinkin' about that land out there. They're concentratin' on *you*. If a man ever got himself two prime enemies in a hurry, it was you tonight."

Little Bob would concede the enmity part of what Howard Mather was saying without dispute. He'd already come to the identical decision by himself. But what turned his cold gaze cloudy was what the marshal has said about Bowman and Cromwell attacking his brother and sister-in-law. He stepped over, opened the door, glanced southward, then stepped back again.

82

"Fennelly's coming," he said, and went after his sheepskin coat.

Mather went to the door to see for himself. When he turned back Little Bob was over at the wall-rack eyeing the rifles and shotguns over there. When he reached, Mather said sharply, "Hold it, little brother—or whatever it is they call you—just hold it right where you are. I asked for your word a while back an' I never got it. If that's how you want it, then no guns, and back in the cell."

"You have my word," Little Bob grumbled. "I'll do as you say and hang right close no matter what."

Mather smiled and gestured. "Help yourself to a gun," he said, turned and opened the door as Brice came stamping across the snow-choked plankwalk. Brice eyed the way Little Bob was handling one particular scattergun. It was the same weapon he'd shot that BC cowboy with; the same weapon Marshal Mather had taken from him much earlier. Brice rolled his eyes around at Mather eloquently. The lawman ignored that look. "Put some extra shells in your pockets," he told the liveryman, then proceeded to do the same thing himself.

Brice half-heartedly took some pistol and carbine bullets, pocketed them and looked over where Little Bob was methodically helping himself from a carton of shotgun shells. He didn't say a word.

Marshal Mather went to the door, crushed on his hat and called to the other two. "Come on; button up an' muffle up, it'll be colder'n a widow's kiss out there."

They went outside. At once their breath turned to feathery steam. The breath of the three sleek horses at the tie-rack was also visible in the stinging cold. Up and down the roadway there were lights showing. It was a pretty sight. As Brice grumbled, stiffly mounting up, "It's pretty all right. Pretty damn' cold. Hey listen, Howard; how d'you know Cromwell won't have his whole blessed crew out here tonight? Hadn't we better round up some more men?"

"Naw," mumbled the lawman, and reined northward up the roadway.

CHAPTER ELEVEN

THEY HAD TOWN A HALF-MILE BEHIND THEM BEFORE Little Bob said, "One question, Marshal: Why me?"

Mather's answer was candid. "Two reasons. One; I didn't want to risk leavin' you back there while I was gone. Bowman looked murder at you, Bob. He's not above sneakin' back into town tonight. You'd be hard to miss, inside that steel cage, an' I don't want any murders committed, especially right in my jailhouse."

"What's the other reason?"

Mather turned and thoughtfully gazed at Little Bob. "Well," he retorted. "This one's not so easy to put into words. Let's just say I don't want a big crew with me tonight, because in the snow like this, we'd be visible for a mile before we even got close. But still, I need a couple of men I can rely on to do what they're told, an', if it comes to a fight, who know how to do that also."

Little Bob drifted his gaze on past, where Brice Fennelly was hunching along on the lawman's opposite side. Fennelly didn't see that glance but Marshal Mather did. He softly grinned at Little Bob, wagging his head.

"Don't worry about Brice," he said. "I know what kind of an impression he leaves with folks, but I happen to know a lot more about him than you do. You're

84

thinkin' he's a coward; that he maneuvered you folks into doin' his fightin' with Cromwell for him. Well; that's right enough. But he didn't do it because he's scairt of Cromwell, although he tries to give that impression all right. He did it because ol' Brice's a great hand at tryin' to get other folks to do his work for him." Mather's strong white teeth shone in the murky evening. "I've had this whinin' old goat at my side a time or two before, in scrapes. He'll do just fine."

Little Bob rode along looking dubious, but he said no more for a long while. Meanwhile, although it wasn't actually late, the world was dark above and white below, giving the impression of full nighttime. And it was icily cold, too; a kind of cold that worked down inside men's coats and mufflers to turn the flesh blue and taut, and to make their joints mildly ache.

Now and then where the ragged clouds were torn, stars as white as ice showed through, but if there was a moon up there they never saw it.

Coach tires and horse-tracks had chewed through the snow of the roadway making an irregular pattern of darkness over the congealed earth. Their horses' shoes crunched steadily along, breaking through with each step. On their left the low-rolling hills looked glisteningly white. On their right where the land was less rolling, there was an endless flow of mottled land, barren where a few clumps of scrub-oaks grew, dark where sage and buckbrush and chaparral huddled in low clumps, but otherwise undisturbed white as far as they could see.

Behind them the pinpricks of Newton's lights blinked out one by one as they rode farther away, until eventually they were entirely alone in a hushed, white world of intense cold, where the only movement aside

85

from their own was being made by those ragged old dirty clouds scudding along overhead, low enough in places to seem possible for a man to raise an arm and touch them.

Brice removed his gauntlets, made a smoke, lit up and blew a grey cloud that disappeared almost as quickly as he exhaled it. "Fine night," he muttered through stiff lips. "I always make a point out of ridin' out in the first blizzard of the year." He looked blankly across at his companions, then waggled his head in rueful disgust. "A feller doesn't have to be crazy, but it sure helps. Howard; you figure to ride up to the cabin? How do we know Reuben won't fire on us by mistake?"

"We'll come in from three different directions," replied the peace officer. "And no matter who fires on us—it'll sure prove I'm right about Bowman and Cromwell figurin' this'll be the right time to make trouble: With me at the jailhouse guardin' my prisoner. An' my prisoner sulkin' in his cell."

"An' me," put in Brice Fennelly, "at my room down at the barn sittin' by the stove like any sane, sensible person should be."

Howard Mather grinned and dropped a slow wink over at Little Bob.

They came into familiar country. Little Bob, with his scattergun balanced across his lap, tried to make out lights, but there were none, at least not yet. He muttered something about the distance being too far yet, and when Howard Mather turned to ask what he'd said, up ahead a gunshot sounded flat and hollow in the black-and-white world.

Mather said, "Hold up!" The three of them reined back. Brice tossed away his smoke and let his right hand rest lightly upon the frigid steel butt-plate of the

Winchester carbine under his right saddle-fender.

For as long as they sat there, nothing happened, but when Marshal Mather eased out and growled for the others to come along, another of those hollow, flat gunshots echoed through the icy hush. This time, though, the lawman kept right on riding. It was Little Bob who called for the next halt. He pointed westward where the rolling land flattened into a long trough through some uneven low hills.

"Up through there," he explained, "will fetch us in below the house."

"One of us," corrected the lawman. "Brice; you know the country over yonder. You peel off from here. Try to get up within rifle-range, but hide your horse somewhere an' go the last few yards on foot."

Fennelly nodded. "Be happy to," he said grumpily. "Walk up out there through fourteen lousy inches of wet snow." He turned and walked his horse off the road. The other two heard him swearing when the horse demonstrated reluctance about wading over where there were no tracks.

Mather balanced a decision in his mind then said, "Let's go. We can get up as far as the next knoll before we have to split off."

They went that far, listening closely for more gunfire as they rode, and hearing none at all. When they halted the last time Howard Mather said, "Sure a strange kind of a fight up there. Folks firin' one bullet each, every fifteen minutes."

"My brother wouldn't be one to waste bullets," murmured Little Bob.

"I reckon," said the lawman dryly. "My impression is that your brother wouldn't push for a fight under any circumstances."

87

Little Bob shook his head. "That's wrong. Rube'll fight. He'll just try his damnedest to talk trouble away, first. But he'll fight."

Mather wasn't listening; he knew the lay of the land also. If one of them went westerly from where they now sat their saddles, and one rode on northward, up the stageroad for perhaps a mile, then also left the road and went westerly, that should put all three of them somewhere beyond the log house and barn. He explained his idea to Little Bob, then said he'd go up north and cut back down to come in behind whoever was out there in the night shooting at the cabin.

"You," he told Little Bob, "remember what you promised back at the jailhouse. You do exactly as you're told. Now then; break trail to the west. That'll put you between Brice an' me—when I get back around behind 'em out there. Don't shoot until I either yell for you to, or until you hear me open up. You got that?"

"Yes."

Mather eyed the tall, rugged younger man a moment, then nodded his head. "Head west," he ordered, gigged his own mount and went northward up the stageroad.

Another of those rare gunshots exploded off in the brittle, westerly night. For almost two minutes there was no reply. When it eventually came, the three men from town were all close enough to hear the muffled echo, which meant this last shot had come from inside the house, or inside the barn.

Little Bob let his horse mush on without guiding it until he came into a shallow dry-wash with the close-in shoulders of the rising hills on each side, then he picked up the reins heading for a particular place.

There were trees in a fold of the hills. Not very many and neither tall nor aged; just scrub-oaks with their

88

shaggy bark and unkempt appearance. Here, Little Bob dismounted. From this place on over to the buildings wasn't very far. The problem was—it was bare ground every foot of the way. Normally at night this wouldn't have posed much of a problem; tonight, with white snow lying everywhere, any dark movement would be visible for a long distance.

Little Bob solved that the same way the Indians solved it; he cut a sage bush off near the ground, grasped the spiny limbs in one hand, grasped the scattergun in his other hand, and started with infinite caution to inch around the base of the low hill where he'd left the horse.

Two-thirds of the way on around and he could see the house and barn. There were no lights, but then he hadn't really expected any. He shoved his bush into the deep snow, squatted behind it, and made a slow, long study of the surrounding night. A gunshot erupted. Now, this close, it no longer sounded hollow. Now it sounded business-like and lethal. More than that, though, Little Bob had no trouble at all spotting the red flash of muzzle-blast. He was over beside the barn, whoever he was. Bob hoisted his bush and started ahead another hundred feet. As he stopped again, the rifle from inside the house roared and bucked. Bob heard Reuben's bullet hit hard against the front of the barn a long yard east of where that sniper stood, down the south side of the barn.

At that distance Little Bob's shotgun was worthless. He had his sixgun under his coat, but even for the forty-five with its six-inch barrel, the distance would be rather great. He started ahead again, angling along so he would come into another little shaggy grove of more scrub-oaks. He settled into that shadowy place and stood straight up; there were enough mottled shadows to completely camouflage him.

He had a perfect view of the house, the barn, even the corrals and the yard. But he couldn't see that man down the far side of the barn. Nor, for that matter, could he see anyone else, either at the house or elsewhere.

While he was straining, a gunman let fly from north of the barn, which meant there were at least two attackers. But in Little Bob's opinion, they weren't making much of an attack of it.

More harassment, he told himself. Cromwell and Bowman, perhaps, and not really trying to do any more than frighten Eulalia and worry Reuben. It struck him odd that Cromwell should be out there; the wealthy cowman hadn't ever struck Bob as the kind of man to do this nocturnal kind of dirty work, personally.

Then a third gunman let fly from just inside the barn's front opening, and Little Bob had to revise his thinking. Now, there appeared to be three attackers. Perhaps, too, there were still more. Reuben answered with a shot from the house. Little Bob shook his head. Rube was waiting too long each time; by the time he'd fire back, those gunmen out there would be fifty yards away in a new position.

A man's gruff call rang out in the unnatural silence. Deputy Marshal Mather had gotten into position somewhere out there in the snow. "Let 'em have it, boys," he cried out, and promptly emphasized that statement by driving a bullet across the yard and inside the barn. Little Bob heard that slug flatten against an unyielding log in there.

From southward Brice Fennelly opened up, but Brice wasn't miserly with his shells; he fired, moved a little, fired again, and did that three different times.

Obviously, the liveryman was trying to create the impression that he wasn't alone down there. The man alongside the barn shot back at Fennelly's last position. He must have come close because Brice let go with three very rapid shots, every one of them slashing into barn-siding across the yard where that invisible gunman still was.

Little Bob heard the man floundering over there in fourteen inches of snow, trying frantically to get away. Marshal Mather concentrated on the inside of the barn. Only once was his antagonist in there able to jump forward, shoot, and jump back again. After that, the peace officer kept him from getting anywhere near the door again with steady firing.

Brice called out to no one in particular. At once, a man down near the out-back corrals fired at the sound of the liveryman's voice, and this was precisely why Fennelly had done that; to locate a target. He blazed away at the shooter.

Little Bob hadn't fired a shot. He was too far away for his scattergun to be effective. His sixgun could've reached the barn with no difficulty, but as the fight began to turn more hot and savage, Little Bob was content for the time being just to watch.

Marshal Mather sang out again. Southward, Brice Fennelly shouted back. Little Bob was silent. Over at the barn a man's rifle barrel being dragged over rough wood made a distinct sound. Immediately, Marshal Mather cut loose towards that sound. Little Bob thought the lawman must have come awfully close, because there was no more firing from the barn.

The silence suddenly returned, deeper and more unnerving than before. Little Bob thought he knew what the BC men were doing. He left his trees, took up his

91

sage bush again, and got down to the farthest limits of the yard where they'd piled some cedar fenceposts. From that spot he could see inside the barn. There was some feverish activity over there. In the reflection off the snow he could make that much out, but nothing more.

Fennelly opened up once more, using rapid-fire. Bob figured the way the muzzleblasts were aimed, and decided Brice was firing at something down behind the barn which he could not see. Then he heard them; at least three mounted men breaking out the rear of the barn in a wild rush westerly. Bob threw caution to the wind, jumped up and charged straight across the empty yard to the front of the barn. He sighted the last horsemen out the back of the barn and let loose with first one barrel, then the other barrel. The rider threw out both arms, dropped his carbine, but clutched at the saddlehorn and raced away.

CHAPTER TWELVE

BRICE FENNELLY AND HOWARD MATHER CAME trotting up. They had also seen the attackers depart. Little Bob turned and said, "Go on over to the house. Tell my brother they're gone. I'll be along directly."

"Whoa," growled the deputy marshal when Little Bob started walking. "Where d'you think you're goin'?"

Bob turned. "Out back. I winged one of 'em. I want to have a look."

"Fine," agreed Marshal Mather. "Brice; you go on over an' tell the folks at the house there's no more trouble. I reckon I'll just stroll along with Brother Bob, here."

They went down through the barn, out through the rear doorway the same way the attackers had exited, then Marshal Mather let Little Bob do the quartering back and forth, up and down, until Bob said, "Here it is, I was sure I saw him drop it." He was holding up a Winchester carbine. Mather came over, took the gun and held it close to his face a moment, then said it was too infernally dark out there to see anything, providing there was anything about the saddle-gun worth seeing.

They quartered a little longer but there was nothing else to be found so they went back inside the barn. Over at the house an inviting, bright lamp was glowing. The good, mildly acrid scent of oak wood in the stove came into the barn too. Mather said, sounding a little glum, "I didn't figure on them getting away. I thought sure the three of us could come up with at least one of them alive an' kicking."

"We still can," Little Bob retorted. "Find the man with buckshot in his back and he'll point the way to the other pair."

Mather studied that a moment then said, "You're plumb sure you hit one?"

Little Bob pointed to the carbine in the lawman's hands. "He threw out both arms and dropped the gun, then he doubled over like he was goin' to fall off, an' made a grab for the mane or the saddlehorn. I hit him all right, Marshal. I hit him damned hard."

Mather turned to gaze over at the house. "We'll see that your folks are all right," he said, "then maybe we'd just better ride right on over to the Cromwell Place."

"Poor night for riding," mumbled Little Bob, turning to stride over to the log house.

As Howard Mather stepped out to keep abreast, he

said, "Bob; for what we've got to do, there never is a *good* night."

Eulalia showed the strain of the siege but by the time Little Bob and the deputy U.S. marshal got inside, her husband and Brice Fennelly had effectively reassured her the peril was past. She was at the stove when Little Bob walked in. She turned and smiled. Reuben came over to say, "You always had a knack of turnin' up at the right time." He gave Little Bob a light slap on the shoulder then extended his hand to Marshal Mather.

"Two trips out here right recent," Reuben said. "At least this trip I was right glad to know you were out there."

Mather nodded, eyed the preparations Eulalia had made to feed them all and said: "Yeah. Well folks, we can't stay so don't go to any bother about feedin' us and all."

Brice looked indignant. "Anything wrong with a man havin' a cup of java to take the frozen curl out of his toes?" Fennelly didn't wait for an answer from Marshal Mather, he walked over where Eulalia was pouring, made a little bow, and picked up a tin cup.

Little Bob walked over also. Finally, since he had no alternative, the lawman also secured a cup of coffee. But he wouldn't sit down. The others did—with their boot-soles raised to the merrily popping iron stove—but Howard Mather drank standing over near the door. He hadn't had time to examine that carbine until now, so he raised the thing up and held it forth so the lamplight would strike it. Big Reuben wandered over to gaze at the weapon. Mather explained how they'd come by the thing. He turned it over. Someone's initials had been burned into the stock with a thin object of some kind; perhaps a heavy, cherry-red piece of wire.

"J.D." muttered the lawman. "Could be anyone; John Doe, Joe Doaks, Jack—"

"Jute Daily," said Reuben. "Li'l Bob; have a look."

They all looked, including Brice Fennelly. Mather asked who Jute Daily was. Little Bob told him. He told him a few other things too, and wound it all up by stating that Jute and Texas Harkins maintained the southeasterly BC cow-camp up until the critters were all drifted nearer the home place to winter.

Mather gazed at Brice with raised eyebrows, but Fennelly didn't know Jute. "They come an' go," he said indifferently. "Maybe if I seen this one I'd know him, but by his name—no."

"Finish the coffee," Mather told them, and set the example by downing the last of his, taking the cup back over where he could thank Eulalia, then returned to the door. Brice lingered over the last of his java, but Little Bob seemed as interested in riding over to BC as the lawman also was.

Reuben said he'd go too. Even Brice was against that. "It's not more men we need," he said to the large man. "It's some July weather." Still, Reuben went out with them while they stamped through the snow after their horses and came together again down by the barn. He offered to fetch them some jerky but they declined that too, saluted and rode off.

The clouds were breaking up; it was late. It was also bitterly cold, but at least the weather seemed not to be getting any colder, and in a minor way that was a kind of a blessing.

Where the stars shone through, the three horsemen had no difficulty picking out the disturbed snow where three hurrying riders had plunged away from the Tollman place. In fact, when Marshal Mather had ridden

95

a half mile and the tracks went directly towards their predictable location, he said, sounding disgusted, "Hell; a brace of ten-year-old kids wouldn't have left this obvious a set of prints."

Brice said, squinting ahead, "Unless they wanted a damnfool lawman to come along with his nose on the ground, an' ride straight into a bushwhack."

That didn't seem entirely logical, and yet it was a possibility, so they alternately watched the tracks, and eyed the roundabout drifts and bare patches.

The land began to improve. At least there were protected places where despite the previous very heavy snowfall, grass and earth still showed. There were more trees too, and sharper cut-banks where cattle could quietly stand and wait out a bad storm. It wasn't snowfall or rainfall that shrunk critters; it was the driving wind, icy cold, which made them hump up. Sometimes one of those whirling white northers would start cattle to drifting; they'd get frost over their snouts and sometimes freezing their eyelashes together so the beasts stumbled along and fell off cliffs or got piled up in shallow canyons where, in the springtime thaws, rangemen would find them down there, tight-packed as sardines, and dead.

BC range had none of those places. Additionally, it was an ideal place for wintering cattle in a country where cowmen figured on losing as many as fifteen and twenty per cent each winter. The three riders who were crossing it now knew the range. Howard Mather said as he swung both arms, "If I had a set-up like this one more lousy section more or less wouldn't make me miss any sleep."

Brice had his own ideas. He said, "That's exactly why you don't even have that one section, Howard," he stated. "To get ahead an' stay ahead in this world, you got to think business day an' night. You got to plan all the time. You can't never make such a remark as you just made; but more important, you dassn't even *think* like that."

Mather grunted, blew on his hands, pulled his gloves back on and said a trifle caustically, "Brice; if being a rich man'd ever meant that much to me, I'd never have put on his badge. But it doesn't. I'd trade places with no man, and Brice—maybe before this night's over, you wouldn't either, 'cause all the land an' livestock an' money in Montana isn't goin' to save Benton Cromwell —if he's what I think he is."

Little Bob let those two pursue their argument a little longer, then he growled over at them. "You fellers ever hear the fable o' the fox who made fun of the turtle? He got to laughin' so hard over the turtle's stupidity he wasn't lookin', an' fell off a cliff."

Mather turned his head, looking right and left. "You see something?" he asked, "or are you just bein' funny?"

"Neither," Little Bob muttered. "Just tired of listenin' to you fellers."

After that they mushed along without a word passing between them until Little Bob halted, tipped back his hat and leaned in the saddle watching the way those faint-lighted tracks went right on down the far, low slope of the landswell he and the other men were sitting upon, and pointed.

"Cromwell's place."

He dropped his arm without making any move to ride on down there. Howard Mather sat a moment, also studying the yonder buildings. "Light in the bunkhouse," he said, which he didn't really have to say since they

97

could all see that little orange glow down there.

Brice made another smoke and lit it. He held the cigarette under his palms warming himself, while he shook his head from side to side. "Too easy," he told the others. " 'Course, if this Jute Daily's hurt bad, maybe Mister Cromwell didn't care about leaving those tracks for us to follow. But if I've got Cromwell and Bowman sized up right, this may *look* like we've got everythin' all neatly wrapped up and tied—but we won't have. Something'll fall through."

"Thanks," growled the marshal, scowling. He evidently took Fennelly's remark as some personal aspersion; conceivably this was the result of their earlier dispute. Brice looked a little surprised. He dragged in off his smoke, lustily exhaled and fell to studying those buildings down there, looking small and dark and functionally square, in their snow-setting.

"You got thin skin," he muttered, still not looking at Howard Mather. "Li'l Bob; what you reckon we'll find down there?"

Bob lifted his rein-hand. "I only know one way to find out," he exclaimed, and started riding down the long, gradual slope. There wasn't a tree or a brush clump until they got within a mile of the Cromwell place, and by then, if someone was bundled up down there, keeping watch, he'd have seen them sure.

Where the land began levelling off Howard Mather said, "I'll ride on ahead a little ways. Whether they see who I am or not, at least when I call out they'll maybe think twice before shooting."

Brice had a comment to make about that, too, but he didn't make it until Mather was pushing his horse onward, leaving Fennelly and Little Bob riding side by side back there.

98

"Fat lot of good that badge'll do underneath his coat, an' if someone down there decides to shoot first, who's to say it wasn't an accident?"

Bob was silent. He kept watching Mather out there plowing ahead towards the lighted log bunkhouse through fourteen inches of churned snow. There would be a sentry, he was confident of that. Men as wily as Cromwell and Bowman wouldn't attack like they'd done back at his brother's claim, then hightail it for home leaving tracks a child could follow, then not expect to be followed.

He was correct. Marshal Mather was nearly a hundred yards ahead, and less than that distance to the onward ranch buildings, when a man called out down there, his voice bell-clear and distinguishable in the crystal-frigid night air. But that sentry hadn't been challenging the marshal; he'd been calling to someone else.

Mather halted, pulled out his Winchester and sat there waiting. Just before Little Bob and Brice got up to him, he hailed the buildings.

"Cromwell! Bowman! This is Deputy Marshal Howard Mather. I'm coming in. I want to talk to the pair of you!"

Little Bob was ten feet back when he said, "Marshal; it might set them off seein' me like this. Maybe I'd better wait out here."

Mather shook his head without taking his eyes off those onward buildings. "You come right along with Brice an' me," he said, sounding gruff. "If they get set off, believe me they'll wish they hadn't." No one answered Mather's shout. In fact; nothing moved down there at all; nothing changed. Mather eased his horse forward. "Let's go," he growled.

It wasn't a long ride, but in some respects, as Brice

99

Fennelly afterwards dryly said, it was the longest ride he'd ever made in his lifetime.

A big dog barked but didn't bound out through the snow to see who the riders were, which made Little Bob think he was probably on a chain.

They reached the edge of the yard. There, Mather drew rein one more time. "Bowman!" he called out. "This is Howard Mather. Come on out!"

Bowman didn't appear. No one appeared, in fact, and Little Bob could see that the lawman was getting angrier by the minute. He jerked his head, rode on across through the dirty snow and halted for the last time at the tie-rack in front of the lighted bunkhouse. He had his Winchester balanced forward, pointing directly at the bunkhouse door.

"Brice," he said, "go over and kick the door open."

Fennelly eased forward to dismount. From the side of the building a shadow materialized, walking slowly. "Won't be no need for that, Marshal," the shadow said. "Besides, we got a hurt man in there; the noise might upset him."

Little Bob recognized the shadow. Texas Harkins. The Texan recognized Little Bob too, as he came on over and said, "Get down an' come on inside, Mister Cromwell's in there."

Brice dismounted first, then Howard Mather. The last man down was Little Bob. He began unbuttoning his coat as soon as he was on the ground, which afforded him ready access to his sixgun, but when he started forward to enter the bunkhouse, he had his shotgun lying lightly in the crook of one arm.

100

CHAPTER THIRTEEN

THERE WERE THREE RANGERIDERS IN THE BUNKHOUSE, as well as Benton Cromwell. There was someone else in there too; the handsome dark-haired girl from the restaurant in town. The one Little Bob had exchanged looks with. She was seated on the edge of a bunk bent over, working upon the blood-flecked back of a man who was lying face down, both arms above his head, naked to the waist and hanging on with a grim grip to the rough posts which formed the supports for his wall-bunk.

The room was hot; too hot in fact, and also it was stuffy. There was a pan of boiling water atop the iron stove over against the back-wall, and a powerful scent of boric acid and salt in the air.

Those three rangeriders who were standing near the girl watching her work on the wounded man, turned, their faces flushed from the heat, and stonily gazed upon the newcomers. Benton Cromwell, still wearing a sheep-skin coat and trousers wet to the knee, also turned. He gave Marshal Mather look for look.

"Late for you to be riding out," he said stiffly, and the peace officer nodded his head without commenting. Cromwell flicked a look at Brice Fennelly, then flicked a longer, harder look over at Bob Tollman. "You're not too particular about whom you ride with, Marshal."

Still Mather said nothing. He stepped over and looked down. "Shotgun pellets," he said quietly. "Tell me, Mister Cromwell; is that man's name Jute Daily?"

The closed-down faces raised towards Mather. Even Sarah Cromwell looked up, finally; looked from her

101

father to the lawman, then on over where Bob Tollman was standing.

Cromwell said, "That's right; his name's Jute Daily. What of it?"

"I'm right interested," drawled Mather, straightening back. "Who was he ridin' with tonight, Mister Cromwell ?"

"Riding with, Marshal? No one. Jute's been right here since midday."

Mather clasped both hands behind his back and stared at Benton Cromwell for a long while, making his seasoned guess about why Cromwell had told that bald lie. "Is that a fact?" he murmured. "Tell me, Mister Cromwell; how did Jute pick up all that buckshot in the back?"

Cromwell turned, picked up a shotgun which was conveniently leaning against the nearby log wall, and handed it over. "One of the boys was cleaning this thing," he smoothly said, as Mather took the scattergun in both hands, "and it accidentally discharged just as Jute walked in front of it."

Mather didn't break the gun right away; he just held it, looking sardonically at Benton Cromwell. You didn't call a man like Benton Cromwell a damned liar in a room full of his own people, with nothing to back you up but a conviction that he *was* a liar.

Mather broke the shotgun. There was a loaded barrel and an unloaded barrel. But the unloaded one still had an empty shotgun shell in it. Mather snapped the gun closed, set it aside, and turned to watch Sarah Cromwell work on Jute Daily's puffy, punctured back.

"Very good," he murmured, and no one in the room was sure whether Mather was referring to the deft way Sarah was doing her unenviable work, or whether he meant the slick alibi Benton Cromwell had engineered. He looked around. "Where's Ned?" he asked.

Cromwell said, "We parted in town after we visited you at the jailhouse. He's either still in town, Marshal, or maybe on his way home. I don't know which."

Mather unbuttoned his coat, loosened his muffler, lifted his hat and resettled it atop his head. He reached into the basin of pinkish water at Sarah's elbow, found a pellet and drew his hand back to study the little lead particle. He held his hand out towards Cromwell. "Buckshot?" he asked.

Cromwell looked, then nodded. "Buckshot," he said blandly.

Marshal Mather slowly smiled. " 'Difference between buckshot an' birdshot," he said, pocketing the pellet. "Mister Cromwell; you didn't have time enough, I reckon, what with us pushin' after you over the tracks you left."

"Time enough for what, Marshal? What are you talkin' about?"

Mather reached, picked up the shotgun he'd previously leaned upon the wall, and threw it. He wasn't smiling now. Cromwell caught the weapon. "Time enough," Mather snarled, "to use your head, Cromwell. The two shells in that gun you say shot Daily by accident are charged with birdshot. It says so right on the casings. Those pellets your girl's pickin' out of Daily are buckshot. It's quite a bit bigger."

For five seconds no one moved. The three BC cowboys seemed at a loss about what course of action to take, so they took none. Benton Cromwell stood like stone, starting at Howard Mather. He moved his right hand and Little Bob Tollman's shotgun dropped down; one of the hammers eased back with a sharp, mechanical sound. Cromwell turned his head and stopped moving his hand. He and Little Bob stared straight at one another.

Brice Fennelly had his right hand out of sight under his coat, but if he was gripping his sixgun no one could see him at it. Another five seconds went past. Marshal Mather said, "Keep right at it, Miss Sarah. Those things'll fester up big as an apple if a feller keeps 'em under his hide too long." Mather turned back towards Benton Cromwell. "You know what I think?" he said softly. "Mister Cromwell; I think you're a damned liar!"

Under any circumstances those were fighting words. But that shotgun in the hands of the lanky, rugged-looking man standing in front of the door, was a powerful dissuader. No one, including Benton Cromwell, moved as though to take exception.

Howard Mather walked completely around the rigid cowboys and knelt down over there so he could look into Jute Daily's grey-sweaty face with its locked-down jaws and eyes swimming with pain. "I fetched your carbine back," he said amiably. "It's had some bullets fired through it tonight, Jute, but you're lucky; you didn't hit anyone. 'Course; in the eyes of the law that's not good enough to get you off scot-free, but it sure could've been a lot worse for you. This way, when I lock you up an' forward the warrant so's you'll have a trial for attempted murder, trespassin' with intent to commit great bodily harm, shootin' at a woman, firin' on an officer of the law, maybe all you'll get is ten to twenty years in the Territorial prison over at Deer Lodge." Mather's sardonic eyes brightened with a little smile. "On the other hand, Jute, you got the right to turn State's Evidence, which means you just might get off free as a bird, providin' you tell exactly what's been happenin' around here for the past six months or so, and particularly, what happened over at the Tollman ranch tonight."

Jute rolled his pain-racked eyes and pushed his face into the blankets, still gripping those two rough posts in front of him. Sweat ran in rivulets. Mather stayed down a moment longer, then stiffly got back upright with a little sigh. As he arose Sarah Cromwell spoke for the first time. Her voice was deep and rich, but right now it had an edge as sharp as the words she uttered.

"What do you do now, Marshal; put him on a horse and make him ride back to town with you, because he wouldn't say what you wished for him to tell you?"

Mather took the rebuke with a little smile. "No," he murmured. "Sarah; we've always been friends."

"Yes," the handsome girl said, drying her hands on a towel. "You and my father were friends too, Marshal."

Mather's smile faded. He raised his eyes. Her father was still under Little Bob's shotgun and wasn't moving. "Something I never liked in folks," Mather drawled, speaking to the handsome girl while looking straight at her father. "Lying."

Sarah turned. "Are you sure he *is* lying?"

Little Bob spoke up. "He's sure, ma'am, and so is Mister Fennelly here. And so am I sure. This gun I'm holding is the one that put those buckshot into Jute. What surprises me is that a woman as handsome as you would side with a liar."

Sarah swung around. "Even if he happens to be my own father?" she shot at Little Bob.

His answer was soft. "No. I reckon I'd feel more contempt for you if you didn't stand by your kinfolk, all right. But that doesn't change anythin' where your pappy's concerned, ma'am. He's still a liar."

"Can you prove that, Mister Tollman?" she icily asked.

105

Bob lowered the hammer on his scattergun, put the weapon aside and placed both big hands upon his hips, all before he made any attempt to answer her. They stared bleakly at one another the length of the half-lighted, half-shadowed bunkhouse, then he said, "It should not be too hard, Miss Sarah. Move away from the bunk and we'll see if maybe Jute doesn't want to talk after all."

Her large eyes widened. "You're a savage," she breathed at him. "Jute is sick; he's badly injured. You wouldn't—"

"Just get away from the bunk," he repeated. Then, aside to Brice, he said, "You can use my scattergun if you wish. Or use your pistol. The first man to move—"

"Wait a minute," broke in Howard Mather, beginning to look surprised at Tollman, and also annoyed with him at the same time. "Just who the hell you think you are, boy? *I'm* the law here. *I* decide what's to be done."

Bob gazed at the lawman. "Then decide," he said. "You have one liar here an' if you wait too long Jute'll be lyin' too. My way, we'd have the truth in five minutes an' could start back with the prisoners."

Cromwell jerked his head around, towards Howard Mather. "I preferred charges against Tollman," he said. "If you let him out of jail, Marshal, you're breaking the law as much as—"

"Shut up," snarled Mather. "When I need someone to explain the law to me, it won't be you."

One of the rangeriders who was standing slightly behind another cowboy, made a slight move. With astonishing speed Brice Fennelly's cocked gun appeared, aimed at that distant man's middle. Over there, a sixgun dropped to the floor.

Brice said, "Howard; we better disarm these folks."

106

Little Bob didn't wait for the marshal's reply to that, he walked over and disarmed the two cowboys still wearing guns, from in front, and he looked each man straight in the face. Afterwards, he stepped around Sarah and crossed to Benton Cromwell. He didn't reach for the cowman's gun, he simply held out his hand.

"Take it," growled Cromwell, but from over by the bunk Marshal Mather snarled right back: "Hand it to him!" Cromwell obeyed.

Bob went over by the door, dropped the guns and reached for his shotgun again. Marshal Mather was darkly scowling; he had a problem. Obviously, unless they commandeered one of the BC wagons and a stout team, they couldn't take Jute Daily back to Newton with them. Also just as obvious was the very excellent possibility that the second Jute could straddle a horse Benton Cromwell would hand him a hundred dollars and point west. Even taking Cromwell in wouldn't change anything; Ned Bowman was still around, and if Cromwell was locked up, Bowman would still serve the Cromwell interests. On the other hand if he took in Bowman *and* Cromwell, he might risk leaving Jute at the ranch for a day or two. The alternative, as he saw it, was just as bad as losing a prisoner; leaving Brice and Tollman at the ranch, the only men with guns, would be inviting bad trouble too.

He gazed around. On Cromwell's side there was nothing but grimly silent and veiled hostility. Those men over there, even without their weapons, were dangerous. Worse still, Ned Bowman was loose somewhere, and Ned *was armed.* He'd come back to the ranch, wherever he now was—and Mather didn't for a moment believe Bowman hadn't also been in that attack on the Tollman place. The way he had it figured it was

Bowman, Jute Daily, and Benton Cromwell.

Little Bob said, "Brice and I'll stay until you can take Cromwell in an' lock him up, then come on back with a wagon and a few more riders."

Sarah looked at Little Bob with smoldering hostility. "You might regret that, shotgun-man. For instance— how do you know I don't have a gun?"

Little Bob's crystal-grey gaze went up and down the tall, handsome girl. "If you do have," he drawled, "you'd sure better be a right smart shot with it, ma'am, because if you've got one—an' you miss me with it— I'm goin' to take you across my knee with a rawhide switch."

Sarah's cheeks reddened. She swung towards her father and the deputy U.S. marshal. "Don't let that man stay here," she said. "Marshal; if you don't take him with you I won't be responsible."

Mather stroked his chin thoughtfully, turned and said, "You're her father," to Benton Cromwell. "Take my advice an' tell her not to be cute while you'n I are on our way to town. He wouldn't cut her in two with his riot-gun, I'm fairly certain, but I sure wouldn't bet a lead dollar he wouldn't do the other, if she give him good cause."

Cromwell said, "Are you taking me in?"

Mather nodded. "Takin' you in, then I'm goin' to come back with a wagon for Daily, an' I'll bring back a few lads to sort of lend a hand at huntin' down Ned Bowman, because once a man lies to me, I just naturally don't believe anything he says, which means I don't believe Ned's in town at all."

Brice Fennelly said, "Howard; Bowman could be outside right now waitin' to bushwhack you."

"Funny we should both be thinkin' the same thing,"

108

said the lawman. "Brice; open that door. Mister Cromwell walks out first, then I walk out so close behind him that if Bowman's out there waitin', he'll have to shoot through Cromwell to get at me."

Fennelly opened the door looking doubtful about this. Mather drew his sixgun, cocked it, shoved it into Cromwell's back and said; "March! Don't slow down or stop or do anythin' silly."

They left the bunkhouse close together and Brice closed the door, dropped the bar into place, forlornly shook his head and resumed his position covering the other BC men with his sixgun. They all of them stood silent until they heard two horses heading out of the yard. Evidently Bowman hadn't been waiting after all.

CHAPTER FOURTEEN

TEXAS HARKINS ASKED LITTLE BOB IF IT WOULD BE all right for him to give Jute a little whisky in a tin cup. Bob nodded from over by the door. For several minutes the only activity was across at Daily's wall-bunk as Harkins got some liquor down his pardner's throat.

Little Bob asked Sarah Cromwell if she was through with Daily. She said that she'd gotten all the pellets out. She also said she didn't intend to bandage his back because it would be handier, for washing him, and also because the healing process would be expedited by fresh air.

Little Bob studied the handsome girl. He put aside his shotgun, thumbed back his hat and said, "Put on that sheepskin coat hangin' on the wall, Miss Sarah." She looked around at him, surprised. "Go ahead, put it on," he repeated, and when she persisted in looking puzzled, he went over, took down the coat and held it for her,

109

from behind. She finally put the coat on. Little Bob walked to the door and nodded his head at Brice Fennelly. "We'll be back directly," he said, then opened the door and jerked his head.

Sarah frowned, making no move to cross the room. Little Bob stood waiting a moment, saying nothing. He and the tall girl stonily regarded one another, but eventually she started towards the door. Texas Harkins said, "Don't go, Miss Sarah." Texas was roughly watching Tollman when he said that. "I wouldn't trust that long-legged sod-buster any farther'n I can see him, ma'am."

Bob stepped aside to let Sarah walk out first, then he threw a scornful gaze at Harkins, saying, "You got reason not to trust me, cowboy. You'n Jute both. You two are too damned dumb not to get caught every time you try something sly." He went out into the bitter cold, closed the door, and stepped off the bunkhouse porch to where Sarah Cromwell was standing, holding the coat tight with both hands while she gazed up at the suddenly clear sky, and took down several deep breaths of the invigorating night air.

She didn't turn nor lower her head as she said, "What is it?"

Little Bob towered above her even though she was tall for a girl. He said, "Beautiful night; sort of lonely and—"

"That's got nothing to do with why you wanted to talk to me," she snapped, turning.

"No ma'am, it sure doesn't. But after that stuffy bunkhouse and the dirty job you had to do in there, I thought . . ." He shrugged, bracing against the raw rancor in her stare, and let it dwindle off unfinished. "Tell me something, Miss Sarah; why? Just because we're outlanders; because we settled on land you folks

110

have been using? Or is it because you cow-folk just naturally don't like farmers?"

"Take your pick," she said coldly. "You've named some of the reasons. There are others, too, why cowmen despise your kind. Because you people steal beef and horses, fence off water and run cattle where you have no business."

Little Bob shook his head at her. "We don't own any cattle. We only have four horses. We've never fenced anything and we don't have to steal food." He looked at her a long moment. She was even more attractive up close. "What sense does all this make?" he asked. "We own that land; you folks are not about to harass us off it, and gettin' that tomfool cowboy killed by sendin' him over to make off with my horse was just plain stupid."

"Are you accusing us of—?"

"Yes'm. Of stealing my spotted-rump horse. And tonight my brother an' sister-in-law were in that cabin when your paw and those other two shot into it."

"Mister Tollman; believe me, if my father shot at your brother he wouldn't have missed."

"He didn't want to hit anyone, ma'am. It was just more of this harassment. So far all it's accomplished is to get one BC cowboy killed, your paw locked up, and make you an' me enemies."

"We would have been enemies anyway!" She turned her back on him and raised her eyes to the cold stars again. "That day in town—you struck Ned for no reason! "

"The best reason I know of," said Bob, contradicting her. "You were across the room. You didn't hear any of it. Maybe Bowman and your pappy told you some story, but believe me, your rangeboss was right lucky he didn't get killed."

She turned back, showing contempt. "By you? Mister Tollman, you're not in the same class with Ned Bowman. If you hadn't walked off, when he got up again he'd have killed you."

Little Bob turned thoughtful and quiet for a time. He too, looked at the high sky, then down at her lovely profile. "He'll get the chance, if that's what he wants. Your pappy too, ma'am. I never ran from any man. All I came out here to do was ask you—why? What's so awful about emigrants that we can't just sort of live side by side out here? You folks don't need that little chunk of Montana at all, but my brother and his wife *do* need it. They need it harder than you ever needed anything in your life. Harder, I hope, than you ever have to need anything. They had a little boy—Jonas—he died of the fever down the Missouri River, longin' right up to the day he died to see what Montana looked like. Miss Sarah; you don't know what our kind of folks need more than anything else—home. You've always had that. Well ma'am. I hope right hard you never have to know what that kind of longin' is."

He stepped back from her. She turned around, fully this time, and looked up into his face with the animosity gone, with her liquid large eyes turning soft. "Wait," she said quietly, then, as he stopped moving, she seemed to have forgotten what it was she'd meant to tell him.

" . . . Ma'am?"

"I'm sorry. I didn't want to be rude just now, but it's been a bad night. A bad week, in fact."

"Yes'm," he agreed. "It's been a bad half year over at our claim. But you got to understand something, Miss Sarah; When folks've been homeless as long as we've been, they'd rather die right in their own yard than hitch up and move on again. It makes it hard to

112

understand, when folks like you with everything to live for, have to concentrate on breakin' folks who have nothing."

"But you were troublesome," she murmured, sounding only half convinced this was so.

He shook his head at her. "No ma'am; the first time we met your pappy and your riders, they looked down on us. Well; we've run into that before; we didn't say anythin' about it until the cattle started driftin' over on to our feed. Even then, we held off. But that was a mistake; I reckon your paw and that Bowman feller are the kind that don't understand it when folks don't want to fight back."

"All right," she said so softly he scarcely heard. "All right, Mister Tollman. I understand."

"Do you ?"

She looked up, nodding at him. "Yes. I know how it all happened because I saw it happen before with other emigrants. But no shooting the other times." She jutted her chin towards the bunkhouse. "No one gritting their teeth in agony like Jute's doing in there." She breathed deeply and let her breath back out again. "I wonder; would you help me, Mister Tollman?"

"Be right proud to, Miss Sarah. How?"

"Ride into town with me; we have to talk to my father."

Little Bob's expression turned cloudy. "Will he listen? I've got your pappy sized up as an almighty stubborn man, Miss Sarah."

"He's stubborn, but so am I, and up until tonight while I was picking that lead out of Jute's back, I never thought how wrong and senseless all this is. Mister Tollman; if it isn't you folks down there, it'll be someone else. Some other emigrant family. Eventually . . ." She made a little

113

helpless gesture with one hand. "Eventually, someone will get killed. That section of land isn't that valuable. I want to tell my father I've had enough. Either he faces up to what he's done or I'm going away."

Little Bob kept gazing in his impassive way down at her. He didn't say anything. Behind them, in the bunkhouse, they could both hear Brice and the others talking. Down in one of the big log barns a cranky mare squealed and kicked the side of her tie-stall, evidently in retaliation for some minor annoyance.

"I reckon we'd better wait," he said, finally. "Brice could handle it all right, from here, but if Bowman came riding in, things could change right fast."

She turned silent towards him for a while, holding her coat tight-closed and looking down. Eventually she said, "I think I'll ride in anyway," and turned as though to go towards the barn.

He stopped her. "I reckon you'd better wait. Ridin' very far on a night like this . . . If you got bucked off or anything . . ."

She turned back. "I've been riding as long as you have, Mister Tollman. I've been riding into Newton from here a lot *longer* than you have." She cocked her head at him. "Or," she said, "is it something else? Do you think I might be going out to find Ned and bring him back?"

He shook his head. "It didn't cross my mind. I was only thinking that if something happened . . . Well; I'd feel sorry about that."

She kept her head cocked a little to one side while she continued to stand out there gazing back. "Come with me," she said. "Mister Fennelly doesn't need either of us. Then we can come back with the marshal."

He balanced the thought, and shook his head. "I said I'd stay. I better not leave."

114

She turned and walked through the crisp crust of hard snow straight down to the barn. He watched her, troubled with his thoughts and his decision. She'd make it all right, he told himself. But if she *didn't*; he turned, stepped up on to the bunkhouse porch and walked on inside where Brice was sitting upon a cocked-back chair nursing a cup of black coffee in his left hand, while still holding his sixgun in his right hand.

"She's goin' to town," he said.

Brice looked up. "It's kind of late," he retorted, dragging the words out as though bothered by unwelcome thoughts. "There are ten dozen snow-banks between here and there. Why doesn't she wait; Howard'll be back directly? Anyway; her paw's not goin' anywhere. He'll be in the same cell, come morning."

"She said she had to go," replied Little Bob, and across the room where he was slouched over a chair beside Jute Daily's bunk, Texas Harkins turned and spoke.

"Miss Sarah don't take kindly to bein' kept back once she makes up her mind."

"Still an' all," mumbled the liveryman, shifting his attention to Harkins, "it's not like a summer night."

Harkins nodded in quiet agreement, then he said, "Well; let Tollman go with her."

Brice looked up again. "Sure enough," he drawled. "Li'l Bob; you ride on in with her. I'll be just fine right here—as long as the stove-wood an' coffee hold out.

Bob didn't protest, not even a little bit, he turned and went back out into the brittle, white-stained night. When Sarah came riding forth from the barn he was out there in the middle of the yard, waiting.

She walked her mare over and smiled at him. He turned without speaking or smiling back, and started off.

For a while she rode at his side without speaking, then she said, "What did the liveryman say?"

"He told me to go with you."

"And the others?"

"Harkins said he thought you shouldn't go alone. He also said you were bull-headed."

She laughed. It was a pleasant, rich sound in the cold hush of the night. "Not really; only when I know I'm right."

"Bein' right," he drawled, "isn't any guarantee you'll live for ever."

She looked at him with interest. "Tell me something, Mister Tollman; do you ever smile?"

He rode along without answering.

They didn't go back the same way Little Bob and the others had reached the Cromwell ranch, but rather they followed some wagon-tracks over which had been superimposed two sets of horse tracks. The indentations showed that beneath the snow was a road. It led eastward arrow-straight and Little Bob guessed it came out over by the north-south stageroad, where they'd then cut abruptly southward.

"You don't smile," she said, "and you aren't exactly talkative."

"If I have something to say, I say it. That's enough, isn't it?"

She shook her head at him. "That's enough with men, Mister Tollman, but it's never enough with women. Where are you from?"

"Kentucky."

"Did you ranch in Kentucky?"

"Folks farm back there, Miss Sarah, they don't ranch. It's different country."

"The people must be different, too, Mister Tollman,"

116

she murmured, still making her close study of him.

"People," he answered, "aren't much different no matter where you go. They have different prejudices, but that's about the size of the difference."

"Do they laugh in Kentucky, Mister Tollman?"

He turned his face to her. "Folks call me just plain Bob. Mister Tollman was my father; he's been dead a long time."

"All right, Bob. Do they laugh in Kentucky?"

"They laugh," he said, and looked straight ahead again. "When there's something to laugh about. But it's been a right long while since there's been a whole lot to laugh about in Kentucky, Miss Sarah. You're too far away, maybe, but there was a war . . ."

"Not as far away as you think," she said, and didn't push any more questions at him, but seemed to drop down into herself for as long as it took them to reach the stageroad, busy with some private thoughts and speculations.

They turned southward and found the rutted tracks both deep and crusted with grain-ice, so that, as they rode along, the sounds of their coming travelled a long way ahead of them.

CHAPTER FIFTEEN

THERE WAS A MOON IN THE PALE SKY BUT IT HARDLY added anything to the brightness which was reflected upwards from the snowfields below. The brightness, however, was deceptive; Little Bob and Sarah Tollman could see in a generally straight and distant line in whatever direction they looked, but objects up close such as boulders, trees, clumps of brush, were blurred and shapeless even from no farther off than fifty feet.

It was, in short, one of those bizarre wintertime nights when there was brightness all round, but with no sharp visibility anywhere. And adding to this uniqueness was the silence. Each time one of their horses raised and lowered a shod hoof, the sound echoed and re-echoed. In fact Little Bob said it would be a bad night to try and slip up on anyone. Sarah's rejoiner was that from this night on, if she had her way of it, there would no longer be any such need.

Bob asked her why her father attacked the claim. "He never struck me as a man who would stoop to getting caught at something like that, himself. Not as long as he had hired men who'd do it for him."

She didn't have any positive answer, only an idea. "When you shot that cowboy and sent him back tied across his horse, my father was stunned. Emigrants don't fight back. Ned was furious. It was Ned, really, who forced the fight from there on. I think my father was just carried along." She looked over at Bob and swiftly said, "I'm not trying to excuse him or make it appear he was too weak to stop the trouble from snowballing. After all, my father is boss; if he'd wanted to he could've stopped Ned from ordering the riders to harass you folks at any time. But the way all this happened . . ." She looked straight at Little Bob. "Do you understand what I'm saying?"

He understood. "Yes'm, I reckon I know what you mean. An' there's something else: that day in the café when I first saw you . . ."

"Yes?"

"Well; I'll admit it sure stopped me cold when I figured out you were Benton Cromwell's girl, but still an' all—like tonight when I told you to put on that coat

118

an' walk outside—I never really believed you'n I'd end up enemies."

"Not even," she said, "when I was rude, out in the yard?"

"Not even then," he averred. "But if you ask me how I knew, I couldn't explain it. I just knew."

They weren't far from Newton now; both of them realized this although as yet there was no sign of the town. It was actually as though they were the only two human beings on earth, riding through a hushed and endless night of stark cold and utter stillness. Neither of them paid the slightest attention to an onward shadow, lean and crouched, standing well clear of a mesquite clump. Neither of them were looking on down the road in the direction of that shadow; they were gazing at each other.

When the gunshot sounded it was so totally unexpected even their horses were too stunned to shy sideways. Bob Tollman felt a blinding rush of heat explode in his left side, then a lesser warmth went all through him turning every nerve and muscle flaccid. He knew he was falling yet couldn't put forth a hand to break the fall. He heard the sound, even, when his bundled-up body struck the snow-crust, breaking through, but he had no sensation of striking down.

Sarah hit the ground with a little cry rushing past her stiff lips. She twisted towards the mesquite clump where that red flash of gunflame had come from, reached, wrenched out Little Bob's shotgun and fired one barrel without even raising the weapon. Backlash staggered her; she evidently had fired without realizing a shotgun kicked much harder than a carbine.

The second time she fired her legs were braced and slightly bent. That time she heard lead pellets spray through the small leaves and wiry branches of that mesquite bush down the road. She dropped the scattergun, bent to reach for Little Bob's sixgun and had to fumble first with his buttoned coat. That's probably all that saved her. The bushwhacker down there let fly with another bullet from his Winchester. It passed a foot above Sarah's shoulders, and Little Bob, who never quite lost consciousness, dreamily thought she should get flat down otherwise she'd be hit.

She got his sixgun and blasted away twice in rapid succession towards the mesquite. No answering shots came back this time, not for a long while, and when one did finally come it was from off to the east, out where the assassin had evidently left his horse before he slunk down to hide in the brush at roadside. But that shot wasn't even aimed; it sang past harmlessly.

Sarah cocked the sixgun and tracked the ambusher by the sounds his horse made crashing southward through crusty snow, and fired. She had no target in sight, for although she could distinctly hear him racing away, that peculiar bright fogginess prevented her from seeing the bushwhacker at all.

When she lowered the gun it still had two unfired cartridges in it. She was on both knees beside Little Bob, as white up around the eyes as the snow she was kneeling in. She bent over and ran a hand under his coat. It came away warm and sticky. She looked over where their horses had stopped a short distance off, unmindful that she still had his sixgun in her hand. Finally, the shock passed, her mind began working methodically again, and she put his sixgun into her coat pocket where it heavily sagged, then bent down and opened his coat.

The bushwhacker's bullet had been well aimed; if the

same fuzzy visibility which had prevented her from ever getting a good shot at their attacker hadn't also bothered the assassin's aim, Little Bob would have been dead by now. As it was, the .30-.30 bullet had plowed a gory gash alongside Little Bob's ribs making a soggy shambles of his left side. She went to work at once to stop the bleeding, lips sucked flat against her teeth, large eyes almost black with anxiety and pain, and each time she raised her face she saw him looking at her. But he didn't speak; couldn't speak. He was having trouble breathing. The blow had paralyzed him some way, making breathing extremely difficult. He was conscious, she could see that from the expression in his eyes, but he was strangely detached, oddly listless and limp with total shock.

She had to use most of his shirt to make the bandage and because he was surprisingly heavy, she had to rear back straining hard each time she had to move his body to make another wrap with her improvised bandage.

She had no idea how long she worked there, half frozen from the knees down where she knelt in dirty snow and crusty mud. In fact the passage of time didn't occur to her at all, until she was finished with the bandaging and had his sheepskin coat back in place again. Then she sat back breathing hard, gazing into his face. Something in the depths of his crystal-clear gaze made a warm shadow as they exchanged a long look.

She blew upwards to dislodge a heavy lock of her curly hair which had tumbled down, then she said, "I'll get the horses. I don't know how, but I've got to get you into your saddle and down to town."

"We'll make it," he whispered, startling her by speaking.

She didn't move for a minute although her legs were

121

cramped and aching. She put an icy hand upon his cheek, bent suddenly on the spur of the moment and brushed her lips across his mouth. "You bet we'll make it," she whispered, then sprang up and went over where the horses were standing.

He rolled up his eyes to watch, then closed them and gingerly took a shallow breath, the first nearly normal breath he'd been able to take since being shot. Evidently the shock was passing; his body was rallying to its own defense. He concentrated on lifting his right arm. It seemed excruciatingly heavy, but he got the hand up where he could see it. Next, he moved a leg. Both efforts caused spirals of the same sense of white-hot heat to explode deep inside him.

He lay back, slowly returning from the dreamy greyness of near delirium which had held on up until now. Pain steadily throbbed with each lurch of his heart, but it was a dull, cadenced kind of pain, not sharp and constant like other pain from lesser injuries would have been.

Sarah returned leading their animals. She gazed down at him. His body-heat had melted the snow; he was lying in a soggy dark place with mud all around. She bent down to say something and that same heavy coil of her hair tumbled low again. Her cheeks were white but her heavy mouth was cherry-red.

"How will I do it?" she asked him. "How can I get you into the saddle, Bob?"

He weakly rolled his head from side to side. "You can't. Ride to town and bring someone back to help."

"No!"

"Listen to me, Sarah," he murmured. "I'll be better here than astride my horse. Whoever shot me won't be back. You ran him off for good. Anyway; he's probably sure he did what he was waiting out here to do. Ride on in. Take my horse with you. If Marshal Mather's around, fetch him back."

"He won't be in town, Bob. No one will." Sarah suddenly straightened up, turned and looked all around. There was a little clump of scrub-oak out a ways, dark and gnarled in the ghostly light. Without a word she bent down, rummaged for his clasp-knife, then, still without explaining, went slogging out where those spindly little tough oaks grew.

She made a travois for him, using both their saddle-blankets lashed between two poles which were secured to the whang-strings of her saddle. He watched, saying nothing, but when she turned to consider means for rolling him on to the travois-sling, he whispered, "Harkins was right; you're bull-headed."

"I wouldn't be if I didn't care," she answered. "Now try to raise yourself up and ease over on to the blankets."

He instead raised his eyes to study her horse. "You sure that mare won't buck and run?" he asked.

She bent, grasped him under the arms and strained backwards, "Help me," she gasped. "Bob; you're as heavy as lead. I'd never have thought you were so solid."

He had to grit his teeth and fight back the waves of delirium that came up, receded, then came up again, but he made it and eased back with his upper body cradled between the travois poles on their combined saddle-blankets, with his booted feet dragging in the mud.

She bent over him, anxious and troubled. She ran a hand under his coat to see if the bandage was holding. It was. She said, "Hang on, now," and went up alongside her mare. But she didn't mount up; she instead took both reins and started trudging ahead, leading. The mare

123

already had all the weight she could lug, dragging back there through the slush and snow.

It was a long walk. If Sarah could have ridden, the distance wouldn't have seemed so interminable, because, actually, town wasn't very far ahead, but she was fearful of riding his horse and leading her own animal. By walking at the mare's head she had complete control. If she'd ridden and led her mare this wouldn't have been entirely the case.

When she got to the outskirts of Newton it was like entering an abandoned town. Here and there a forlorn nightlight feebly burned. The silence was intense. The cold was freezing her soggy clothing to her body, but the exercise kept her warm.

If there'd been anyone abroad to see that astonishing spectacle as she slogged through the greasy mud of Main Street, leading her mare and dragging the laden travois, they would have undoubtedly been rooted in amazement. But there was no one around.

She headed for the doctor's house, which was as dark as all the houses throughout Newton, tied up at the rack and staggered the last thirty feet to strike the front door with her half-frozen small fist. There was no response so she took out Little Bob's sixgun, reversed it, and struck the door three hard blows with the gunhandle. That time, she stirred up some life. A man's gravelly voice growled for her to wait a moment. She turned to look out where her mare and the spotted-rump horse stood at the rack. When she turned back the door was opening and a shock-headed burly man fastening his belt and looking savage, filled the doorway. At the sight of Sarah Cromwell out there, wet and half frozen, rumpled and with blood on her, the physician's dark look evaporated. She pointed.

"He's on the travois, Doctor, and he's badly hurt. Someone was waiting beside the road. When we rode up, he shot Bob. Help me."

The doctor reached, caught Sarah's shoulder, pulled her inside where warmth rushed over her, then he said, "Sit down before you fall down. I'll take care of your friend."

The physician took down a coat from a peg just inside the door, shrugged into it and went outside. Sarah let her breath out and unsteadily sat down. She wasn't aware that she was still holding Little Bob's sixgun in her hand until the burly doctor came back, staggering under his limp burden, and gruffly said, "You won't need that gun. Put it down and open that white door over there. Then you can help, so don't sit down again."

They got Little Bob into the doctor's dispensary where the medical man lighted two lamps, brought one over for Sarah to hold while he unbuttoned the soggy coat and looked at the soggy, red bandage, then twisted to gaze at the handsome girl.

"Your work?" he asked. She nodded, making a little gesture of futility. "No," the physician said, "I wasn't criticizing, Sarah. It's very good. If you hadn't stopped the bleeding he'd have died from loss of blood. Especially the way you had to drag him in here. Were you two alone when he was ambushed?"

She nodded, beginning to suddenly feel very drowsy and unsteady. "We were on our way to town. It happened about two miles out . . . Doctor?"

"Come along," the physician said, and took her to a couch. "Lie back now."

"I'm muddy, Doctor."

"Well, well; how strange. Now lie back and be quiet."

CHAPTER SIXTEEN

IT WAS NEARLY NOON BEFORE SARAH AWAKENED, AND when she moved she flinched; muscles she hadn't even known she possessed ached with a solid dull painfulness. Little Bob wasn't over there on the doctor's table any longer. In fact, except for her, the dispensary was quite empty. Also, except for the couch where she'd slept, the room had been cleaned up as though two soggy, filthy, bloody, nearly frozen people hadn't even been there.

She stood up. The effort made her wince anew. Somewhere she heard men speaking in low tones. She went to the door and opened it. The voices were closer but still indistinguishable.

She saw a small lavatory off to one side, went over there and washed as best she could, ruefully examined her mud-stiff clothing, then set her heavy head of hair in place and crossed to the closed door beyond which those masculine voices were still speaking.

When she opened the door her surprise was complete. There were four men in there including Marshal Mather and big Reuben Tollman, as well as the physician, but what surprised her especially was the fact that Little Bob was fully clothed and sitting on the edge of a bed, while the others were standing along the walls or were sitting on chairs.

They stopped speaking the moment she came in. Big Reuben was sitting; he arose at once. The other men looked over at her. The first one to say anything was the doctor.

"You look more or less recovered from last night," he said, walking towards her. "We were just talking about

126

you. About how you brought Mister Tollman in on that improvised travois."

She let the doctor lead her over to big Reuben's vacated chair; all the way across the room she and Bob Tollman looked levelly at one another. As she eased down she said, "You shouldn't be up and dressed."

Howard Mather rolled his head and Reuben joined him in heading for the door. Little Bob caught them just as they were passing through. "Wait," he said. "I'm going with you."

Howard Mather screwed up his face in simulated anguish. "I thought we just went over all that," he exclaimed. "You heard the doc; he says you were almighty lucky an' it's a miracle an' all that stuff—but you're still bled out a little, and weak. You can't go, Bob."

"Go where?" Sarah asked, twisting to look back at Mather. No one answered her. In fact, no one even looked at her.

"Rube," said Little Bob, "fetch my horse up from the liverybarn. I'm goin' with you."

Big Reuben looked troubled. He threw a gloomy look over at the doctor as though appealing for aid. The physician shrugged. "I can't stop him," he told Reuben and Marshal Mather. "I know what's good for him, of course, but I don't think that's ever stopped a man from doing what he feels he's got to do." The doctor turned. "Bob; you were luckier than any man has a right to be. Why push it? Besides, regardless of how you feel after a night's rest, you're still an injured man and you're still weak."

"The horse," said Little Bob, gazing hard at his older brother. "Fetch him up to the tie-rack outside, Rube. I'll be right with you." He stood up. He had a fresh shirt on and his coat was in a corner, dried out now but still showing stiff mud stains. At the door, Mather and Reuben traded an exasperated look, turned and stamped on out of the doctor's house.

"Bob?" Sarah softly said, and afterwards waited for him to bring his attention back to her. "Where are they going?"

"After Ned Bowman, Sarah. He's the one who shot me."

" . . . Ned? Are you sure?"

He eased back down upon the edge of the rumpled bed. "I'm sure. So is the marshal. He thought he'd killed me an' headed for the ranch. Marshal Mather was also makin' for BC, but he took the short-cut instead of the road. When he and the men with him came up, they heard gunfire and charged on in. It seems Bowman *was* in town like your pappy said, only he returned to town after the attack on my brother's place, to wait for Rube or me down there where he could bushwhack us. He figured we'd ride for town and tell the marshal.

"Well; to make a short story of a long one, Mather and his boys from town drove Bowman off when he was tryin' to get your cowmen inside the bunkhouse to jump Brice Fennelly from inside while he kept Brice busy from outside."

Sarah gazed at her hands. They were chapped and red from the icewater and cold of the night before. "Does my father know?" she asked quietly.

"He knows. Rube and Howard Mather told him. So did Brice Fennelly. I reckon, from what my brother said this morning, Brice was pretty badly shaken up by what happened out at your ranch last night."

She raised her eyes. "What did my father say, Bob;

128

does he know what happened to you and me last night, too?"

Bob nodded at her. "He knows the whole story. He said if Mather'd turn him loose he'd hunt Ned down and make him quit."

"And . . . ?"

Bob wagged his head, looking sardonic. "It's too late for that, Sarah. If your pappy got in Bowman's way he'd kill him."

"Ned . . . shoot my father? Bob; you don't know what you're—"

"Sarah; it's me he wants. I flung him out in the dirt on his face and he's wild about that; it happened in front of all the folks who've always sort of looked up to Ned Bowman. If your pappy or anyone else tries to stop him now, believe me, he'll kill them. That's why I'm goin' with my brother and Marshal Mather to run him down. It's got to end with me on one side, Bowman on the other side. If they go after him without me, he'll double back. If they corner him, he'll kill them if he possibly can—not because he cares a tinker's damn about them—but so's he'll be able to come back and get me. I don't want to end it like that. There's already been too much pain and injury. He wants me for humblin' him, an' I figure I owe him his chance, so I'm going with Rube and Howard Mather. You understand, Sarah?"

She nodded, her eyes brightening suspiciously. "I understand, Bob. Only . . ."

He arose, crossed over, scooped up his coat, shrugged into it and turned to the physician. "Keep her here, Doc. She's had a bad time of it lately. Keep her here an' make her rest." Bob strolled on over, halted in front of Sarah and put forth a big hand. "No broken ribs even," he said. "And eight-inch gash sewed up like a Christmas turkey, an' a little lost blood. Sarah; I owe you a lot."

She took his hand and squeezed it, hard. She stood up and leaned against him not even aware that the physician was in the room with them. "You take care," she whispered. "It's going to be a bad wait, for me."

"Go down an' talk to your father."

"Yes."

"An' if it gets too bad, ride out an' see Eulalia; she's Rube's wife. There never was a woman quite like Eulalia."

She reared back and gazed upwards. " . . . Never?"

He bent and brushed her lips with his mouth, then stepped back. "Up to now there never was."

"Now there is?"

"Yes'm. Now there surely is."

He walked out of the room without looking back. Sarah and the physician gazed after him. The doctor shook his head a trifle sadly, then said, "Well, Sarah; when you can't change 'em I'd recommend pulling for them—hard."

She nodded, not trusting herself to speak.

There was a bright sun shining, the skies were as clear as pale blue enamel and a glare rose up off the snow to make men pinch their eyes nearly closed as they sat their saddles out front of the doctor's building, briskly talking.

Marshal Mather explained how he'd come on to Ned out at the ranch. "He'd have got Brice sure," he told Little Bob, "if those BC riders in the bunkhouse with him had decided to take Bowman's part. But they didn't; in fact they didn't do anything, so Brice was still holding Ned off when we got out there."

"Where's Brice now?"

"Down at his barn mad as a wet hen. He doesn't blame you. In fact, he told me he sent you back with Miss Sarah. But all the same he refuses to come along this time." Mather shrugged. "I can't blame him."

"We won't need him," said Little Bob, feeling his left side beneath his sheepskin coat. The bandage was tight and dry. It was also thick, as though the doctor had padded him with gauze or cotton, beneath the cloth. "Where is Bowman now?" he asked.

Mather didn't know, but he said, "He left tracks out there. We'll hit them and keep goin' until we find him."

Reuben looked up and down the sunlighted roadway. "That was last night," he rumbled. "Bowman's had four, maybe five or six hours to get a long way off."

Mather didn't dispute that, he just said, "Won't make a damn, friend. It won't make a damn. When I track a man like Ned Bowman, I stay on it until I get him. He's a lousy bushwhacker. That's the worst kind of a louse in my book." He lifted his hand. "Let's go. And Li'l Bob—I think you're crazy as a coot. I know that won't turn you back, but when the pain gets bad, just you remember I think you're crazy as a coot for trying this in your shape. We might not get into a town again for a week."

"An' maybe we'll be back tomorrow, too," replied Bob, turning his horse to join his brother and Howard Mather as they went slogging up the northward roadway.

There were riders out for the first time since the blizzard had struck. There were even some wagons heading overland for Newton from the outlying ranches, evidently to take on a load of provisions just in case another blizzard struck. It was this fresh stirring of life that gave the manhunters what they badly needed.

131

They encountered two cowboys riding south with bedrolls behind their cantles, wrapped in blanketcoats, and with mufflers up over the tops of their hats, down beneath their chins, and tied like that. They were Arizonans, they said, when they stopped in the roadway as Marshal Mather and the Tollman brothers rode up, and they'd had all of Montana Territory they wanted. Furthermore, as far as they were concerned, if the white men tried to give Montana back to the redskins, they'd strongly advise any decent Indian not to accept.

One of them then said, just casually. "An' we ain't the only ones pullin' out. You boys know that feller who's old Cromwell's rangeboss; that dark, ornery lookin' cuss—I can't rightly recollect his name—well anyway; we seen him packed for a long ride too, about two hours back, headin' east on that trail that leads out to the Salt Sink."

"Bowman," said Howard Mather. "You talkin' about Ned Bowman?"

"That's him," crowed the Arizonan. "We never really knew him. Just been on a few mid-summer roundups when he'd come over with a crew to take back the Cromwell critters. An' he was bundled up for ridin' too, Marshal."

The Arizonans would have sat and talked longer but Mather jerked his head at the Tollmans, said "Adios" to the Arizonans, and spurred his horse over into a steady little mile-eating lope on up the mushy roadway. He didn't slacken speed until he came even with a fresh set of tracks going easterly between some snowed-over wagon ruts.

"You boys know that country out yonder?" he asked, not acting too interested in the answer he'd get. "No? Well; there's a big greasewood prairie out there folks

132

call Salt Sink because of the salt deposits in the middle of it." Mather pointed to the sifted-over wagon ruts. "That's the road. Cattlemen use it to haul salt back to their cattle. If Bowman went that way he's got a real good chance of gettin' away, after all."

Little Bob strained to see far out. "Why?" he asked.

Mather raised his rein-hand to ride on. "Because," he brusquely replied, "there's nothing out there but mile after mile of the meanest, most desolate brush country you ever saw, flat as the palm of your hand so'd we'd never be able to even get close to him even without this snow—with it, he'd see us coming miles before we even got within rifle range."

"Then we walk him down," said big Reuben. "Bob and I've done our share of that kind of huntin', Marshal."

Mather moved out, following Bowman's tracks. "Yeah?" he growled. "'You ever do it when the game you was stalkin' could shoot back?"

The sun was good across their backs and shoulders, and because they rode slowly, Little Bob's wound didn't bother him at all. Still; the farther they went the more it became clear that what Howard Mather had said back in town was likely to be proven true: before they hit Newton again, or any other town, chances were excellent that they'd have been in the saddle for a long time.

Reuben finally said, as they came out of the rolling country and got their first good look at the enormous flat prairie ahead of them, called Salt Sink, "Marshal; why don't we just go back and you can telegraph an' write ahead giving Bowman's description?"

"Because he's a bushwhacker, that's why," muttered the lawman. "I never give up on that kind, Reuben."

"Even if Little Bob wouldn't press charges, Marshal?"

That remark brought Mather's scarred face around looking thunderous. He glared a moment, then said, "Reuben; if you don't like it this way, go on back. You too, Bob. I'm goin' to bring in Ned Bowman if it's the last thing I ever do!"

Bob, also scanning that huge stretch of snow-covered flat emptiness, wryly thought it just might be the last thing Marshall Mather—and he and his brother too—ever did, for even if they found Bowman, and got him, if it started to storm again out in this forlorn, forgotten stretch of nowhere, the chances were good none of them would ever even be found until the following summer, and even then he had his doubts. This Salt Sink country was as desolate and empty as any land he'd ever seen. Chances were excellent that riders crossing it, even in summertime, wouldn't be the kind who'd ever mention finding three dead men and three dead horses.

CHAPTER SEVENTEEN

HOWARD MATHER KNEW THE SALT SINK COUNTRY. He pointed out two landmarks. One was where a train of freight wagons had been ambushed, everyone killed, the mules, weapons and freight-goods stolen. The other landmark was where a man and his bride had made a blissful camp one night, and the following morning discovered their horses had gotten away in the night.

"Wandered about three days, I reckon," recounted Mather. "When we found 'em they were shrunk down to nothin'. It was August an' there's no water out here in summertime."

Little Bob kept swinging his head. As he reasoned

aloud to the others, as immense and flat as Salt Sink was, even a man with two or three hours' start should be visible, especially with that virginal blanket of white over everything.

"Sure," agreed the lawman. "These tracks we're following will take us to him. At least they'll put us where we can *see* him. But the danger is that he'll see us first. After all, he sure knows by now he's bein' hunted. Li'l Bob; he thinks he's wanted for murder. There's no more dangerous fugitive under the sun than a man who figures he's already lost. That kind'll fight like a buffer cow at calvin' time just for another few hours on earth. We'll see him all right. What's botherin' me is how that's goin' to take place, an' where we'll be when it happens."

The answers to Howard Mather's questions were a long time being answered, and meanwhile the bright sun which was coldly shining, began to turn filmy. There were no clouds; at least not in the general sense of the term. It was a pale, diaphanous kind of overcast which came to dilute the sunlight, and if it fooled the men from Kentucky it didn't delude Marshal Mather a bit. They were a quarter of the distance out across that huge, empty world of loneliness and snow, when Howard first noticed it. He stopped, lifted his head and looked all around.

"Storm comin'," he announced, quietly. "I was afraid of this." He looked at Bob and Reuben, then twisted in the saddle to consider the raw and lonely miles they had already traversed as he said, "The question is: Have we time to go back before it hits, or should we push on an' hope it'll hold off until we can get across this damned sink?"

"Push on," Bob said. Reuben made no such snap-decision, but then big Reuben was not by nature a snap-judgement-man.

135

He said, "What are our chances of getting off this plain before the snow comes?"

Howard Mather made a wry face and lifted his reins, moving forward again. "Who knows, Rube? That depends on how fast the storm's moving in. If it'll hold off until evening, an' if we don't stop—or get stopped—we can probably make it on across and into the hills on the far side where we could hole up in a canyon—maybe. But if it starts snowin' within the next couple of hours—we're in a mighty poor position."

Having made his point, as well as his personal decision to push onward, Marshal Mather said no more, but from time to time he'd tilt his head and watch the gauziness up there to see how fast it was increasing.

By mid-afternoon there came a little icy wind out of the north to stir the topmost layer of snow. Their horses were annoyed by this and occasionally blew their noses, but aside from inconvenience, the wind didn't slow them any.

The sun by this time had a huge pale circle around it, and the last of its brilliance died slowly making the world an eerie place of bitter cold, endless snow, and very real peril for the three horsemen who were dwarfed to less than ant-size by the land they were plodding through.

They halted once, out where a thin rivulet of snowwater offered both men and horses a chance to pause and drink. The water was so cold, though, they could take down only a few swallows. Two miles onward from that place they found a ten-foot-square area where a mounted man had gotten down to stamp around getting his sluggish circulation moving again. Little Bob thought that was a good sign but neither his brother nor the deputy U.S. marshal were much encouraged by it.

For one thing the lawman was becoming increasingly concerned with the weather, for now there were some ominous black clouds sweeping in low over the northern rim of their lost world, and that little low wind was dying down to an occasional gusty blow which whipped up the snow. Another thing which seemed to trouble Mather was the distance they had come. They were roughly in the middle of the sink; on ahead stretched a monotonously deadly landscape identical to the land behind them.

But they kept going, and so did the tracks they were following. It was near three o'clock with daylight beginning to be influenced towards early darkness by those scudding dirty clouds, that Reuben said, "I smell smoke."

Such a possibility in this woodless, snow-covered country was so remote Howard Mather looked at the elder Tollman as though he thought the cold was affecting him.

Little Bob drew rein, lifted his head and slowly turned it from left to right. Mather started to grumble. Bob said, "He's right, Marshal; take a deep breath with your nose pointed southward."

Mather did, his expression reflecting doubt and exasperation. He took another deep breath, and another. Then he straightened in the saddle saying, "It can't be. There's no wood out here."

Reuben started his horse off, leaving the tracks they'd been following. "Maybe there can't be, Marshal," he muttered, "but there *is*."

They turned southward with Howard Mather looking both perplexed and troubled. "We'll lose him if we don't stay on his tracks," he grumbled, without making any real effort to turn back and follow the tracks.

137

"Maybe the wind's blowin' that scent up-country from a long way off."

Bob said, "You know bettern' that," and concentrated on the gloomy world ahead of them, where the brightness was leaving the sky to be replaced by an ominous, cloudy gloom.

They rode for a half-hour, all the time with those wisps of wood-smoke scent in their faces, before something else came to distract them. It was a soft, steady flow of warm air coming straight against them out of the south. Howard Mather at first refused to believe their good luck, but as that warm air kept increasing until it grew up into a constant, gentle blow, he finally lost some of his tenseness.

"Chinook," he said, sounding so enormously relieved the other two men looked over at him. "Chinook wind, thank the Lord. If it'll just keep up, at least now we won't get buried in a blizzard or wind up ridin' around in circles blinded by snow."

Neither Reuben nor his brother had ever had any experience with Montana blizzards except the one they'd recently come through back in the Newton country, so they didn't know what was so clearly distracting Howard Mather from their pursuit of Ned Bowman. The law officer saw their expressions and wagged his head at them.

"Let me tell you boys somethin'," he explained. "A killin' snow can start this time of year with no more warnin' than we've already had; a haze over the sun, sudden silence all around, a few black clouds—then snow. Days on end of it. Folks caught even a mile from home can get lost and freeze to death in a matter of hours. When you've lived in this country as long as I have, you'll know what I'm talkin' about. I've come so

138

close a couple of times it scares me just rememberin'."

That warm southerly wind, though, did something else; it diluted the smoke-scent they'd been following until they lost it entirely. Mather considered this problem, then said they should split off, each one riding farther out and parallel to the others.

"There's no danger," he told them, "as long as we keep each other in sight. But it's goin' to get dark soon, so close inward as you go, an' that way we'll always be able to see each other."

Little Bob angled off to the right, Reuben rode out to the left. Mather remained where he was. In this manner they continued their southward sweep. And their tactic proved successful, in the end, but for a long time, with darkness increasing, none of them had much hope this would be the case.

What helped was a little lull in the warm wind. Immediately, Little Bob caught that smoke-scent again and wigwagged with his arm for the others to angle over more in his direction. They did so, letting their horses pick the course through heavy snow, neither pushing the animals nor encouraging them to go any faster than a plodding walk, for everything now depended entirely upon their animals.

They began to encounter gentle dips in the land, which indicated they were getting away from the heart of Salt Sink. Little Bob changed course several times because he lost the smoke-scent. The last time he did that was where a diagonal gully intersected the range on a crooked angle, running about northwest to southeast. That time, too, was where he got the smoke-scent very strong. Then the warm wind brisked up again, and didn't slacken off again for the balance of the day.

Those ominous black clouds were spreading out and

thickening, back up in the sooty north. There was an odd iron-like smell to the air as though hot and cold were meeting somewhere behind them far off where the northerly cold front and the advancing chinook wind from the south were coming together in the roiled overhead atmosphere.

Marshal Mather was hunched low swinging his arms, reins looped, when Little Bob suddenly halted out there to the west and raised his hand high in the air, rigidly still. At once the lawman grabbed up his reins and also halted. He twisted to throw a warning gesture over at Reuben. All three of them sat perfectly still until Little Bob slowly lowered his arm and beckoned.

They came together on the far side of a low landswell which looked to be a solid, heavy wall of snow, but which wasn't solid at all. Twenty feet ahead and visible despite the failing light, were fresh horse tracks. They seemed to come out of the frozen west and they angled around to the far side of that onward low roll of snow-covered land.

"We found him," said Bob quietly. "Just over this rib of land." He lifted his head, sniffing. The smell of smoke was stronger than it had ever been before.

Howard removed his gloves and rubbed his hands briskly together, all the while studying the roundabout country. He knew every yard of it, so he said, "It looks to me like the darn fool got scairt out there on the prairie and turned back, but in such a way that he'd always have low hills to protect him." Mather pointed southwestward. "He's led us in one big circle. The stageroad's yonder, and southward lies Newton." Mather went back to reviving the circulation in his stiff fingers and said, "It never once occurred to me he'd leave off heading straight across the Sink."

140

Little Bob also removed his gloves and rubbed his hands. He didn't have his shotgun with him, and there was no carbine in his saddle-boot, so he fished beneath his coat and tugged forth his sixgun. Marshal Mather watched, and shook his head.

"He'll have a carbine, Bob. You try'n get close enough to use that thing and he'll cut the top off your head six times before you get off one shot."

Mather dragged out his own carbine. Beside him, big Reuben reached down and tugged his weapon from the boot also. It was another double-barrel shotgun. Howard gazed at the gun, at Reuben, and gave his head a wry little shake. "Looks like I'm elected," he muttered, loosening in the saddle. "Rube; that scattergun won't even reach as far as Bob's forty-five."

Reuben wasn't perturbed. Without replying he dismounted, winced from the prickles of pain that shot upwards from his half-frozen feet, and stamped life back into his extremities.

When all three of them were on the ground Marshal Mather checked the loads in his Winchester then reached down to professionally tuck the lower portion of his sheepskin coat under his shell-belt on the right side, exposing his sixgun for easy access.

Reuben surprised both Howard and Little Bob by what he did next. Stepping to the near side of his saddle he fished inside the saddle-pocket and drew forth a crumpled white sheet. Without heeding the others he flicked the thing out, swung it around his mighty shoulders and tucked it into his coat. Howard said, in a low outward rush of astonished breath, "I'll be damned."

Reuben's reply to that was practical. "Yes you will— both of you—if you try skulkin' around this hill lookin'

141

the way you look right now." He pointed. "I'll go around from the left. You two can crawl up over the top if you like, or go around from the right." Reuben patted his scattergun. "Don't worry about me, Marshal, or my shotgun. We'll get close enough."

Mather's gaze began showing a fresh respect for the larger man. He obviously was thinking some different thoughts about Reuben, and Little Bob, noticing the lawman's altered expression, said, "I told you he'd do, Marshal, if he had to."

Howard nodded and turned back to studying the sky, the landform up ahead of them a few yards, and the country beyond, as much of it as was visible from where they were standing.

"If he's got a lick o' sense he'll surrender, but I'm not real hopeful of that, boys," Mather said, standing in snow almost to his knees and looking straight ahead. "I'll tell you one thing; he can shoot. In a way I even dislike the idea of announcin' we're out here by givin' him the chance to quit." Mather shrugged. "But we got to do that."

Reuben adjusted his sheet. Except for his neck and head, he blended perfectly with the countryside. It was turning grey everywhere now except underfoot, and that also helped Reuben's disguise. He broke his shotgun, checked the loads, snapped the weapon closed and nodded, then started mushing ahead and to the left of the onward landswell.

For a moment Bob and Howard Mather watched him go, then the lawman softly said, "When a feller doesn't fight, I usually figure he's got some yellow up his back. This time, I reckon I was about as wrong as a man can get.

"I told you," stated the younger Tollman. "He'll fight; he just hates doing it."

CHAPTER EIGHTEEN

THEY WORKED ALONG INTO POSITION, ALL THREE OF them; Reuben to the left of the rib of snow-covered land, Marshal Howard Mather and Bob Tollman to the right. As they were creeping around their westerly slope a yard at a time, Mather said, "A cowboy with a lick o' sense will always try an' put a hill between him an' the north, in this country. All the bad cold comes out of the north. But this time it sure didn't help, did it?"

Little Bob didn't answer. He was in front, his full attention fixed on the curving shoulder of land they were inching around. Once, he halted to listen. A horse around there blew its nose and stamped. Another fifty feet onward Bob halted again. This time he and Howard Mather distinctly heard someone around there beyond sight breaking wood. Mather shook his head. "There's no wood in this country," he said.

Bob finally got down in the snow and crawled. He had to break a trail, which was slow going. Howard Mather came along behind him using the younger man's tracks. The aroma of burning wood, even diluted by that warm wind which was steadily blowing now, became very strong. Bob halted and gently eased down in the snow. Behind him, Marshal Mather swerved to crawl up closer, then he also lowered himself.

There was a saddled horse around there in plain sight, and the way it was standing told an eloquent story. The animal was "pointing" with his left front leg. He was, in other words, holding that front leg out in front of him so that actually none of his weight rested upon it. The beast obviously was lame. He'd perhaps pulled a tendon by stepping into some snow-covered hole out on the sink somewhere, or had possibly bucked his shin, but whatever the cause, Ned Bowman hadn't turned back towards the settled parts of the land because he'd been fearful out there on the Sink; he'd turned back because he had to replace his lame horse, and the only way to do that was to get close to a town or a ranch.

The second mystery was solved when they eased a little farther around the slope and caught sight of a wrecked old abandoned wagon. That was where Bowman was getting the wood for his little fire.

Mather grunted in his throat about that, satisfied with this clear solution to something which had been stumping him for a long while.

But they couldn't see the fugitive. He was back up against the south slope of the landswell, evidently. They couldn't even seen his fire, although the aroma was all around them by this time.

Mather muttered. He was wondering about Reuben. Bob told him Rube would be in place by now, so the lawman said he hated to throw away their surprise-advantage by hailing the fugitive, but that even a bushwhacker deserved one chance to throw out his guns.

Little Bob turned, craning around the slope. He was privately debating the feasibility of crawling still closer; perhaps of even getting close enough to tackle Bowman by hand. The peace officer guessed his companion's thoughts from the way Tollman was leaning out and peering. He said, "Forget it. You're too big to burrow through the snow. He'd see you sure, an' I already told you—Ned Bowman can shoot. We'll get him even though we have to warn him first. It's just a sort of pity, givin' ourselves away like this."

Bob settled back. His side was beginning to ache

from the cold but he kept his coat buttoned to keep moisture out, which was more important.

Marshal Mather raised up a little, inched ahead another five feet, looked pained, then called out: "Bowman! This is Deputy U.S. Marshal Mather; we've got you cut off. Stand up and chuck away your guns!"

For ten seconds nothing happened. Mather pressed flat down realizing that the fugitive would be able to guess his position from his voice. Little Bob pushed his gun-hand ahead and took a rest in the snow. He and the lawman exchanged a look, then the gunshot came, crashing-loud and vicious, feathering the snow thirty feet in front of Mather.

Little Bob swung abruptly and started mushing his way straight up the slope. It was hard going but his strategy was sound; he proposed to try and get above and behind Bowman while Marshal Mather kept the wanted man occupied from below and to the west.

Like many sound and excellent ideas, this one didn't work either. The reason was simple enough; those ten seconds after Mather had sung out, when he and Little Bob had surmised Bowman was sitting around there by his fire, stunned, had been employed by the fugitive climbing to higher ground too.

He was ten feet above and to the east; he saw Little Bob plowing through snow on all fours, and fired at him, nearly blinding the younger Tollman with snow which exploded in his face where the bullet slashed through.

Bob didn't wait; he turned and hurled himself back down the slope. Bowman fired twice more, each time with his carbine. He missed both times and Marshal Mather put a stop to his gunfire by shooting back up in the general direction of Bowman's muzzleblasts.

145

Little Bob rolled to a stop covered with snow and grimacing from pain. He gasped and lay still for a while, his breath roughening the roundabout air with frost. Then he frantically began to gesture to Marshal Mather. He either couldn't or wouldn't yell out, so Howard had to try and interpret the gestures without help.

Bowman yelled something from where he was flattened in the sidehill snow, then fired again, this time evidently towards Howard Mather. Howard was beginning to crawl away just before that slug struck where he'd been lying until a moment earlier. He looked back, saw what would have happened if he hadn't been moving, correctly surmised that Bowman was high enough up the far slope to be able to look down on him, and sprang up to go sprinting back around the hillside towards safety. Bowman fired twice more then stopped shooting altogether.

Little Bob was under the lee of the hill recovering from his own near-demise, and was safe at least for the time being from discovery. Also, covered with snow as he was, and being motionless, he hadn't much to worry about. He could see Howard Mather around the shoulder of nearest land. Howard was lying out there with his carbine in both bare hands, intently staring up the hill where Bowman would appear eventually, unless he went back down to his horse.

Bob eased up a little, winced, set his teeth and went crawling carefully back around the slope towards Howard Mather. He wasn't thinking of anything except getting into the yonder lee of the hill where he might be able to escape detection long enough to get one fair shot, so when the shotgun blast came, it stopped him still.

He looked downhill at the lawman and Mather looked

straight back at him. There was an agonizing silence after that gunshot of Reuben's.

Finally, Mather took a chance and raised up slightly. When no shot came, Little Bob resumed his crawling ahead. He was panting; despite the fierce cold, crawling through deep drifts of snow was exhausting and overheating at the same time.

Then the carbine cracked again, driving both Little Bob and Howard Mather flat again. Evidently all Bowman had been trying to do since Rube's scattergun-shot was to find Reuben, which, under the circumstances, wouldn't have been as easy as finding Bob and Howard Mather; Rube was the same color as the snow.

There was another carbine shot, this time, or so it seemed to Little Bob, coming from atop the landswell and westerly out along its farthest low ridge. He turned and began a direct crawl up the hill.

Mather sprang up and floundered ahead recklessly until he too was in the lee of the slope. Then he sank down to lie a moment panting for breath. That was the last sight Little Bob had of him for a while.

The silence built up again. Bob was near the top of their hill when Howard called out to Ned Bowman for the last time.

"Ned! You damned fool, you can't get us all! Listen to me for a minute! Your horse is lame, you're on foot, we got you surrounded and outnumbered—and you're not wanted for mur—"

The gunshot came from farther along the top-out; it shut Marshal Mather off in the middle of a word. Reuben's shotgun let loose again, its thunderous roar sending churning echoes chasing each other down the darkening land.

Little Bob got up to the edge of the top-out, lay flat a moment, removed his hat, piled snow atop his head and raised his face up until he could see straight along the ridge. A Winchester cracked again, but it was pointed in the opposite direction from Bob; he guessed that from the sound, and raised up still more. He saw where Bowman had plowed through the snow; saw where he'd turned to crawl eastward towards Reuben, then shook off the snow, put his hat back on and eased up over into Bowman's tracks, moving gingerly eastward along the rim.

Mather evidently had also moved, for somewhere to the east, along the north side of the slope and well over towards where Reuben had to be, a Winchester blasted away twice. Another Winchester farther up, fired back. Reuben's scattergun let fly one more time, this time loosening first one barrel, then the second barrel. Little Bob, realizing his brother would now need reloading time, jumped up on to one knee trying hard to catch a glimpse of Bowman. He saw him!

Bowman was along the far edge of their low hill flat in the snow and angled away facing both north and east. Bowman was pinned down and he was concentrating on catching either Howard Mather or Reuben Tollman. He either didn't believe anyone else could be back there behind him, or wasn't concerned with that strong possibility.

Down the hill and out a ways stood the three horses. Little Bob understood finally what Bowman's strategy had been: Get over the hill, run out to those animals and get away fast leaving his own crippled beast back there for at least one of his pursuers to struggle back to town with.

It was a good notion, Bob thought. The trouble with it was simply that it wasn't going to work. He started walking straight down the rim, sixgun cocked and pointing ahead towards the curled, dark shape in the onward snow.

Howard Mather let fly and Bowman swung to answer back. Down Bowman's far slope Reuben cut loose again with one barrel of his scattergun. Bowman twisted back to answer that blast too. Little Bob was less than two hundred feet off and still slogging silently through the heavy snow.

Mather shot up the hill. Bowman wrenched around to answer. Little Bob halted a hundred and fifty feet away and raised his sixgun. Bowman yanked his trigger down in the general direction of Marshal Mather, and the firing pin fell on an empty chamber. Bowman levered and yanked a second time. His gun was empty.

Little Bob hesitated. He'd been set to kill Bowman a second earlier. Now, he let the pistol-barrel droop a little and quietly said, "Drop it, Bowman!"

The fugitive's head whipped around as his body began to snap up out of the snow. He saw Little Bob and just for a moment, there was astonishment in his eyes, then he swung the carbine as hard as he could, and let go of it.

Bob was standing in something like ten inches of loose snow. He couldn't jump clear so he swung to take the carbine along his uninjured side. The gun struck him on its angling flight and made him stagger, but otherwise it didn't hurt. He straightened back around, gun-hand moving. Bowman was charging straight at him, while at the same time he was clawing under his buttoned sheepskin coat for his sixgun.

Bob fired.

Bowman was leaning forward in his fierce intensity. The bullet seemed to have missed him entirely for he kept leaning, kept struggling fiercely to cross the little intervening distance. Little Bob looked, then recocked his sixgun and raised it one more time. From far back he saw his brother rise up out of the snow. He was directly in Bob's line of fire, should he miss Bowman. He hesitated, trying to move to one side so he could fire and still not endanger Reuben. He never fired that second shot at all.

Bowman reached to within ten feet of him and suddenly lost all his momentum and hung there, eyes bulging, mouth wide open to gulp in the thin, frigid air, then he simply wilted; collapsed and tumbled head-first into the snow at Bob's feet.

Howard Mather was struggling to reach Little Bob too, the same as big Reuben was doing, but for Howard the going was a lot rougher; he had to climb all the way up the hill. Big Reuben only had to stalk across the rim, and Bowman had already trampled the trail up there.

Little Bob stood a moment gazing at the fallen man. He bent down, heaved Bowman over on to his back, yanked open his coat and drew forth the rangeboss's gun. Then he eased off his own hammer, holstered his sixgun and knelt in the snow.

Reuben and Howard got up there; Howard was gasping for breath and leaned upon his carbine staring wordlessly at Ned Bowman.

Big Reuben got down, put aside his shotgun and wiped snow from Bowman's face. "He's going out fast," Reuben said. "Where did you hit him, Bob?"

The younger man shook his head, soberly watching their fugitive's face drain of color. Reuben threw back the dying man's coat. They all saw the congealing spot of blood where Little Bob's .45 bullet had struck Ned Bowman near the breastbone, high up.

Reuben shook his head and gently closed the coat again. Ned Bowman didn't have a chance. Even if he'd been back in Newton at the dispensary, he still wouldn't have had a chance.

They waited but it didn't take very long. When Bowman turned loose and relaxed they lugged him down, tied him on his lame horse, turned silently homeward and didn't say a word among the three of them until, in the bitterly cold white distance they saw the warming sight of Newton's little orange lamps.

Then Little Bob said, "Marshal; I got a question I'd like you to answer."

"Shoot," said Mather, looking tired to the marrow.

"What happens to Sarah's uncle?"

For a hundred yards Mather rode along in thought. Then he lifted his shoulders and dropped them and said, "I reckon that'll be up to you folks, Bob. You'n Rube and Rube's wife are the ones got the short end of all this—leavin' a couple of dead men out of it. Cromwell will have to stand trial; that's the law. But it'll be what you folks say at his hearing that'll determine how things go for him."

Little Bob gave Rube a look. Rube solemnly winked and just as solemnly smiled. Marshal Mather didn't see it, but Little Bob smiled back. Cromwell wouldn't suffer too much, after all, which wasn't really what Little Bob was concerned with; but a man can't marry a handsome girl and at the same time testify against her uncle. He rode all the way back to Newton smiling.

We hope that you enjoyed reading this
Sagebrush Large Print Western.
If you would like to read more Sagebrush titles,
ask your librarian or contact the Publishers:

United States and Canada

Thomas T. Beeler, *Publisher*
Post Office Box 659
Hampton Falls, New Hampshire 03844-0659
(800) 818-7574

United Kingdom, Eire, and
the Republic of South Africa

Isis Publishing Ltd
7 Centremead
Osney Mead
Oxford OX2 0ES England
(01865) 250333

Australia and New Zealand

Bolinda Publishing Pty. Ltd.
17 Mohr Street
Tullamarine, 3043, Victoria, Australia
(016103) 9338 0666